"The National Weather Service has issued a traveler's advisory for today."

Hal leaned closer to the radio, followed by Natalie and Randy.

"I'm sure you're wondering what's been closed," the DJ went on, "so let's get right to it. Titan Tool and Dye, Cumberland Electric, Gearco, the Carousel Mall, the Health Barn . . ."

"He's killing me, Hal," Natalie said through gritted teeth.

". . . the Rotary League Bowl-a-Thon, Saint Mary's Macramé and You Seminar, and finally, the weekly poker game at my house. That concludes the list of closings for today."

Hal couldn't believe it. Natalie slumped up against him. "No," she moaned. "They can't do that to us."

Then the DJ came back on, sounding reluctant. "Oh, I forgot one," he said. "All schools are officially closed for a snow day."

Hal cupped his hands like a megaphone around his mouth. "Snow day!"

Natalie raced to the window to look out over the neighborhood. "Anything can happen."

snowday

A novelization by Mel Odom
Based on a Screenplay by
Will McRobb & Chris Viscardi

A MINSTREL® BOOK

Published by POCKET BOOKS
New York   London   Toronto   Sydney   Singapore

A MINSTREL PAPERBACK *Original*

 A Minstrel Book published by
POCKET BOOKS, a division of Simon & Schuster Inc.
1230 Avenue of the Americas, New York, NY 10020

Copyright © 2000 by Paramount Pictures. All Rights Reserved.

SNOW DAY and all related titles, logos and characters are trademarks of Paramount Pictures.

This book is published by Pocket Books, a division of Simon & Schuster Inc., under exclusive license from Paramount Pictures.

All rights reserved, including the right to reproduce this book or portions thereof in any form whatsoever. For information address Pocket Books, 1230 Avenue of the Americas, New York, NY 10020

ISBN: 0-671-03838-9

First Minstrel Books printing February 2000

10 9 8 7 6 5 4 3 2 1

A MINSTREL BOOK and colophon are registered trademarks of Simon & Schuster Inc.

Printed in the U.S.A.

This one's for the nephews,
John Ross, Justin, Eric, and Wayne,
who are all young enough to truly
appreciate snow days.

Prologue

I guess I've got an overactive imagination. At least that's what my best friend, Lane, tells me. She says I have a compulsion to obsess over things, events, and—oh, yeah—people. Some people more than others.

I keep this journal so I can get all of the thoughts in my head out. They've got to go somewhere because my brain gets crowded sometimes, and I don't like the idea of telling anybody everything I think. Not even Lane. And like I said, she's my best friend. Maybe someday I'll let her read this journal and we'll both have a good laugh.

One of the things I like to think about is snow days. You know, those days when the world seems to come to a sudden stop to catch its breath.

But life is like that, you know? Sometimes you gotta just follow it along to see where it leads.

1

Like I said, snow days are awesome. It all begins twenty thousand feet up, in the middle of a cloud. Two atoms of hydrogen bond with a single oxygen atom to form water. Now, this is where it gets tricky. Something like sixteen different atmospheric conditions have to click for it all to work properly, but when it does and the temperature drops below zero as it often does this high up in the sky, the water crystallizes and a kind of hexagonal miracle occurs.

No two flakes are exactly alike in terms of symmetry, shape, and, more important, taste. My sister, Natalie, chews the snowflakes she catches in her mouth, and she always has this dreamy smile. But when those snowflakes gang up on our town every winter, they always have the same effect.

Visibility drops to zero . . . tires spin . . . roads close . . . wind-whipped monster drifts swallow cars whole . . . and finally, everything in the world comes to a beautiful grinding halt. Then, from the guts of this blizzard inferno, the Lords of Winter emerge ready to seize the day as their own. No school. No rules. No excuses.

It's a day when anything can happen. They have a name for such a day. They call it . . . snow day.

But that's not the way it is now. I can look out the window now and see the sun shining down on the green lawns of Wilkerson Street.

Bruce Hebert, our neighborhood mailman, was out making his rounds a few minutes ago. He

2

pushes a mail cart and always seems caught up in his own world. He's short and squat, and not exactly the friendly sort. Today he was carrying a hand-held battery-powered fan, like winter was over and we were going straight to summer. It was disheartening, to say the least.

But that wasn't what happened. We didn't go straight to summer. I want to write about one snow day in particular. Our story begins in the middle of a winter that almost wasn't. Usually when February rolls around in our town, you start wondering when the winter will finally end. But this year we were still waiting for it to begin.

Mr. Hebert went on delivering the mail the day before that snow day, too. The day before everything happened, a kid dressed as a polar explorer had his sled hitched to his dog and was kind of saying, "Mush," every now and then.

Some said the weird weather was due to a disturbance in the jet stream. Others thought it had something to do with the millennium. Most adults didn't seem too worried. But the kids were. There was an unspoken agreement between winter and them, and winter wasn't living up to that promise.

While I was thinking lots of thoughts I tended to obsess over, my kid sister was out on a mission of her own. She and her friends had staked out Principal Weaver at his house. I won't go so far as to say all the kids in school, or even most of them, hate Mr. Weaver, but sometimes he gives them reason for a strong dislike.

3

And on some days, Natalie blazed trails few dared to follow. She told me what happened later. She and Chet Felker and Wayne Alworth, her best friends, had taken snowballs from the deep freeze, where they kept them for emergencies and special events and put them into a cooler. Then they headed for Principal Weaver's house, next door to ours.

He was in the backyard grilling steaks when they got there. He wore Bermuda shorts, an apron, and a chef's hat. Barky, his dog, sat nearby on his haunches, eyeing the steaks hungrily.

Well, not all of us were waiting for a snow day.

"In the summertime when the winter is high," Mr. Weaver sang, "you can reach right out and touch the sky . . ."

Natalie, Chet, and Wayne had climbed up the back of our house and crossed the roof to a spot where it overlooked the Weavers' backyard. With the snowballs dripping cold water between their fingers, they settled in, waiting for Natalie to give the word.

One thing about my sister, she's got an arm when it comes to snowballs. She threw first, and the snowball smashed into the side of Mr. Weaver's head, staggering him over a lawn chair and sprawling him on his behind. One of the steaks landed on the ground. Before Mr. Weaver could move, Barky seized the steak and ran for the hills. Spatula in hand, his chef's hat kind of crooked, Mr. Weaver glared around at the neighborhood.

Nats already had that covered, though. Our

4

chimney was big enough to hide them all—even Wayne, who's kind of on the pudgy side and has a yellow streak a mile wide. They hunkered down behind the chimney, giggling. At least, Nats and Chet were giggling. Wayne was worrying. That's what he does best.

"Man oh man oh man oh La Mancha," Wayne whispered fearfully. "Principal Weaver. You hit Principal Weaver. We are going to get in so much trouble."

"Get a spine, Wayno," Chet said. "The guy's getting way too cocky. Look at him. He's rubbing our faces in it."

"That clam dip's got to learn that winter's not over until we say it's over," Natalie declared.

But Mr. Weaver wasn't going to give up. He cranked the radio up louder. "Is that the best you got? Is it? Well, how about this?" He raised his voice. "In the wintertime when the weather is fine, you'll be doing long division and memorizing state capitals until you go blind, because there's no snow days, no snow days, no none at all."

"Quick," Chet said. "Let's reload. The man is asking for it."

Natalie checked the cooler they'd used to transport the snowballs. "That's it from last year's stash. I guess we're out until it snows again."

Wayne looked up into the clear sky. "If it snows."

"It'll snow," Natalie growled. She looked up at the sky, but there wasn't even a single cloud there to give her hope. It was just one of those depressing moments. The last snowball was gone, and even though it had been a direct hit, winter seemed to be gone.

While Natalie worried about the fate of an entire season, I had my mind on more important things. See, there was this girl, Claire Bonner. And I guess maybe that's where this story really begins.

Chapter 1

Claire Bonner stood at the end of the diving board in swim class. Hal Brandston thought *every eye* in the pool area was on her. She was cute and athletic, and still had a little tan left over from last summer.

Hal tried to ignore the irritated looks Lane Leonard was giving him. *Okay,* he thought, *maybe not every eye in the pool area is on Claire.* Lane was his best friend and had been for years. They sat in the bleachers at the side of the pool, waiting their turn to dive.

Light flashed from the gold bracelet around Claire's ankle. Even from the bleachers Hal could see the whale-shaped charm that hung from the bracelet. The bracelet itself had her name written in script. Claire always moved with easy grace, making her dives look simple.

With Lane looking at him like he was some lab

specimen, Hal felt like he had to say something to explain his attention. Something philosophical, maybe. "Every dive tells a story, you know. You just have to know what to look for."

Lane rolled her eyes. She could broadcast attitude when she wanted to. Today it kind of reflected in the T-shirt she wore with the upside-down smiley face. And no other girl could roll her eyes quite the way Lane did.

Luckily, Hal had Claire to look at instead of those rolling eyes. So he looked.

"I know what to look for," Bill Korn said. He sat next to Hal. They were both dressed in swimsuits, with their goggles and towels around their necks. Bill was medium-size, same as Hal, but he carried an air of good-natured goofiness around him. He also took girl-watching much more seriously than Hal did. Hal had eyes for Claire. Bill looked at every girl in high school.

Claire ran forward in short steps, bounced, tucked, spun, and sliced the water like a knife.

Hal stared at the water, watching Claire glide effortlessly through it like a porpoise. He tried to ignore Lane's reaction and forget about those rolling eyes that made him think of slot machines he'd seen in the movies.

"Hm," he said, deciding to be philosophical. "Interesting. That dive is telling me that she's looking for a new love in her life. Someone fresh, bold . . . *foxy.*" He was trying to make a joke, kind of lighten things up.

Lane obviously wasn't prepared to have things

lightened. "Hal, Claire Bonner wouldn't spit on you if your head was on fire," she said.

Hal took a little offense at that. "I bet she'd spit on me."

"Definitely," Bill said, trying to take off his T-shirt but forgetting that he had a towel around his neck. He looked like an escape artist at work.

"If she could see you, maybe," Lane said. "But unfortunately, to people like her, people like you are invisible." She glanced at Bill, who was fighting a losing battle with his shirt. "If only *you* were invisible, Bill."

"Huh? What?" Bill mumbled, causing some of the nearby students to dodge back.

Hal turned to Lane, knowing he was treading on dangerous ground. But he saw that Claire was out of the pool again, already heading back up to the high board, and he got kind of brave, one of those two-second bravery things that makes a geek look at a bully and let fly with "You and what army?" when he knows he's about to have his head handed to him.

"So you think I'm invisible, huh?" he asked. "Well, if I'm invisible, then I guess she wouldn't see me when I do this." He boldly waved to Claire. *Dumb idea, dumb idea,* his mind cried out, finally catching up with that two-second bravery. The bad thing was that bravery faded just as quickly as it came.

Claire just kept climbing the ladder to the high board.

Hal's face burned.

"Maybe if your hair was on fire," Bill suggested.

9

It was too much to take. Even Bill was busting on him. Hal pushed up from the bleachers and walked toward the pool. "All right. So I'm invisible. But the day will come when Claire Bonner will finally see just what she's been missing."

To make matters worse, he attempted one of those barefoot slides all the first-string swim team pulled off and made look so easy. But he'd never been first-string. Not even on his best day. The next thing he knew, he careened out of control, windmilling his arms and trying in vain to regain his balance.

Luckily, instead of the floor, the pool was there to break his fall. He plunged in, splashing water everywhere. He gave up and went with it, sinking deeper, mortified to find in that very instant he made eye contact with Claire. She was on the diving board, ready to make her next dive. She stared at him, too.

Hal's original idea was to just stay underwater until he died . . .

. . . but luckily the deep end had other plans for him.

Hal swam out of Claire's way, knowing he wasn't going to hear the end of it from Lane and Bill. A golden metallic sheen sparkled on the grate at the bottom of the pool. There was something familiar about it. He swam down to it, totally curious.

There, on the grate, was Claire's ankle bracelet, a thin line of gold attached to a whale charm. He reached down and took it from the grate, thrilled to see that it was intact and not broken. He stared at

10

the bracelet for a long time, captivated by the promise it held.

"Dude, just go over there and give her the bracelet," Bill said. "This is your big chance."

Hal glared at him, face turning red again. *It's not that easy.* "Don't you think I know that? I'm just waiting for the right moment."

"Right moment?" Lane repeated, doing that eye-rolling thing again. "What? Are you proposing?"

They stood in front of the gym with the other students, all waiting for rides to take them home. Everybody was buddied up into groups of friends.

Claire Bonner, however, stood by herself. She looked at the building across the street, but Hal couldn't see anything that was very interesting. It was just a building that had been there for years.

He glanced down nervously at the bracelet in his hand. It felt heavy and solid.

"Come on, bro," Bill said. "Gut check time. Just walk right up to her, look deep into her eyes, and . . ."

A yellow convertible skidded to a stop at the curb in front of Claire, causing everybody nearby to jump back.

"Get my head beat in," Hal said sincerely. He knew who was driving that car.

"Hey, babe." Chuck Wheeler, football big and summer blond, sat behind the wheel of the convertible. "Hop in. Everyone's waiting for us at the diner."

"Go away," Claire replied.

That brought Chuck up short. But it didn't stop him for long. His voice softened. "Claire bear, what is going on here? You won't call me back, you won't talk to me . . ."

Hal thought he was going to gag. He couldn't believe Chuck Wheeler was acting soft around any girl. Any girl in school would have gone out with him. *Except Lane,* he realized.

Claire faced him, arms crossed, definitely not friendly. "I told you I needed some time to think. About us. About everything."

"What's there to think about?" Chuck asked. "You're Claire Bonner, and I'm Chuck Wheeler. We're America's Dream Team."

That was true, Hal knew. That was how everybody in school thought of them.

Claire groaned and wrinkled her nose as if she smelled something bad.

The crowd around them was more interested than Chuck felt they had any right to be. This was the kind of drama that made rumors around the school take quantum leaps.

Chuck turned on the spectators, and he wasn't sweet anymore. "What are you looking at?"

Instantly, all those people found something else to look at, even if it was only the back of the head of the person in front of them.

Chuck leaned out of the car toward Claire and talked more softly. "What is it this time? If it's about Greg's party last night, I'm sorry. I truly am. But I think it turned out for the best. I do."

"Chuck, you stuffed that kid in the trunk of your car."

A guilty look filled Chuck's face. "He said he needed a ride."

Claire shook her head. "You know what? I'm done thinking about it. We're through. And this time I mean it."

Hal, his breath tight in his lungs, watched her leave. *She's really going to walk away?* When he watched her continue going, a silent cheer filled his mind. *She's really going to walk away!*

Chuck was stunned for a minute. But he made up for it. "You want to end it? Fine!" he shouted at her back. "It's over! *Finito!*"

Claire shouted back without ever turning around. "Oooh, Italian," she said. "I'm so impressed."

"Yeah, well, here's a little more: *Sayonara!*" Chuck put his foot on the accelerator and peeled out of the parking lot.

Hal watched him go, his fist tight around the gold bracelet with the whale charm. Suddenly he felt as if that short length of gold might take him further than he'd ever imagined.

And even Lane can't argue that now definitely isn't the right time to give it back to Claire. He pushed the bracelet into his pocket carefully, making sure it didn't snag.

13

Chapter 2

Quiet as a mouse, Natalie slipped into her brother's bedroom. She knew Hal wouldn't be home from swim practice for at least another twenty minutes.

That would give Natalie just enough time to save the universe. Maybe even save it a couple times.

She stared at the wall of shelves that held all of Hal's action figures. It wasn't so long ago that they weren't on those carefully built shelves protected by Plexiglas.

She walked toward them, taking in all the bright colors, the capes and the masks, the clenched fists and valiant poses. There was nothing like super-heroes!

When she was younger, Hal hadn't wanted Natalie to touch his action figures. But she'd been a baby, losing pieces and occasionally biting the ear or nose off of one.

Then, when she got older, after Randy was born, Hal had kind of introduced her to them. He'd talked about each hero, about their powers and origins, about the things they believed in. And about how each of them had saved the universe.

Saving the universe was something Natalie had kind of planned on in her own life. She just didn't know quite how—or from what.

A few months ago, though, Hal had put the action figures away, not playing with them and not letting her play with them. She wasn't sure what had caused the change in him, but she knew she didn't like it.

She knew what she did like, though. She opened the Plexiglas doors and made her selections. It was time to save the universe.

"You have defied the mighty Meltar for the last time," the heroic voice boomed. "Prepare to taste the flame of justice, Freon."

Hal spotted Natalie in her room as he passed by in the hallway. Then he noticed the action figures she was holding.

She was busy helping Meltar save the universe. At the moment, Dr. Freon, one of the biggest threats in the known worlds, was menacing them. Meltar never went up against any small-time threats.

Natalie used her best villain voice: "How many

times do I have to tell you it's *Doctor* Freon. *Doctor!*" She glanced up and spotted Hal.

Hal frowned, not happy with his sister borrowing his action figures. "Natalie . . ."

"Fangor!" Natalie said in her Meltar voice again. "Thank goodness you're here. Freon has kidnapped our Earth winter." She plucked another action figure from the bed and tossed it to him.

Hal refused to take the bait. "What did I tell you about playing with these guys? They're not toys. They're collectibles." He was a little preoccupied. He hadn't stopped thinking about the scene that went down between Chuck and Claire. He also remained aware of the bracelet hanging heavy in his pocket.

Natalie shifted back to her Dr. Freon voice, and nobody did Dr. Freon quite the way she did. "It would seem your brother is something of a Nimrod, is he not?"

Hal smiled. "That's enough from you, Freon."

"That's *Doctor* Freon!"

"Seriously. Hands off the merchandise, okay? If I'm going to sell these guys, I've got to keep them mint."

"Sell them?" Natalie asked in alarm. "You can't. We're a team. You can't split us up."

"Nats, teams split up all the time. It happens." Still, he felt bad telling her that. He started collecting the other action figures from the table.

"But who's going to defend the universe?" Natalie asked.

Hal didn't meet her accusing gaze. It was too hard. He'd taught her to believe in heroes and saving the universe. "Believe me. The universe will be just fine." He tried to say it so even he would believe it.

As Hal left the room, Natalie disagreed. "No it won't."

Chapter 3

Tom Brandston, the Channel 6 Action Weatherman, wore a Hawaiian shirt, multicolored leis, and a grass skirt that shimmied with every move he made.

It was painful, totally embarrassing.

But Tom was a pro. Grass skirt and fish-belly white legs or not, he delivered the weather report. *"O na lima ha-I ka o-le-lo,"* he boomed with a smile. "In Hawaii that means 'the hands tell a story.' These hands are saying, 'Happy, sunny fun time,' as more unseasonably warm weather wiggles its way into our area. Over to you, Phyllis." He shook the grass skirt, embarrassed at having to do that.

The blond, too-happy news anchor, Phyllis Amlicher, chuckled at him. "Hot weather and a hot body. What more could you ask for?"

Tom smiled sweetly at her. *"Mahuuna owi,* Phyllis."

Phyllis shifted her attention to the camera. "We'll be right back with the story about a Syracuse man who sued himself . . . and won! Stay tuned."

As they went to commercial, Tom stepped off the weather stage, shaking his head.

Tina Stillman, the station's news producer, stepped out from behind the cameras. She wore an expensive suit that fit her exactly. *"Mahunna owi?"*

"It means 'kiss my butt,' " Tom told her, trying to ignore the film crew that passed by and made teasing remarks.

"Will you just relax?" Tina asked.

"I'm a meteorologist, Tina," Tom growled. He grabbed a fistful of grass skirt and shook it at the news producer. "Last time I checked, meteorologists wore pants."

"Oh, yeah, well, the last time I checked, we were the number three station in a three-station market. Translation: we stink. As such we need to provide a programming alternative to our audience. Translation: wear the skirt or hit the bricks."

Tom shook his head in disgust. He and the producer had never really gotten along, and the situation was getting worse.

"I know it's hard on your dignity," Tina said, "but until we find a way to beat Chad Symmonz, we're stuck." She pointed to a bank of monitors that kept tabs on the other local channels.

Chad Symmonz was featured prominently on one of the monitors. He was forty and roguish, and carried on like he was some kind of movie star. He

19

pointed to the super high-tech 3D computer graphic on the screen behind him. " . . . you want to go on a ride? Climb aboard. Ladies, you sit next to me, whoa, as we dip down under the clouds with our exclusive Channel Ten 3D Dope-ler radar."

"*Dope-ler* radar?" Tom grumped to the other weatherman on the monitor. "It's *Doppler* radar, you dope. And what's with that name? How can you take a guy seriously who spells his name like that?"

Tina raised her eyebrows. "I have to say, your jealousy is not a pretty thing to see. In fact, it's sickening." She turned and walked away. "You want pants, Tom? Start getting Chad Symmonz's ratings."

Tom glanced back at her. *"Mahuuna owi."*

Tina froze, then turned back to glare at him.

Tom decided to blaze before things turned any uglier. His grass skirt rustled as he moved.

Later that evening, Hal listened while his dad fixed dinner and told him what had happened at the station. His mom hadn't made it home yet, which wasn't unusual. While Tom put the soup and sandwiches on the table, he talked about the telecast, about what he could do with the equipment Chad Symmonz seemed to take for granted.

They'd waited a little while, hoping Laura Brandston would show up soon. But she didn't. Her marketing job had been taking up more and more of her time. It was kind of a quiet meal. Except for Randy,

Hal's little brother. Nothing was ever quiet around Randy.

Randy was four years old, one of those kids who could outpace and outlast the Energizer Bunny and still have enough oomph left over to walk that little pink critter's shattered bits into the ground. That night, Randy was as active as ever. As they ate, they dodged occasional bits of thrown food.

Natalie didn't even bother to dodge, which made Randy kind of lose interest in her as a target. Hal had noticed she was totally into glum mode. The kind of mood you got into when you had to scrape the floater fish out of the aquarium and do the flush thing. Hal shoveled the food down, trying to clean his plate. He had plans, and he was nervous and anxious.

"Dad," Natalie asked, "is it ever going to snow?"

"It doesn't look good, honey," Tom said. "It's just been tough lately. Last year it was El Niño, and this year it's—"

"El Sucko," Natalie supplied.

Tom chuckled. "El Sucko is about right."

Across the table, Randy slurped his soup through a silly straw filled with twists and turns.

"Randy," Tom asked, "is that how we eat soup in this house?"

Randy paused for a moment, then went back to slurping soup.

"Just checking," Tom stated.

"Hey, Hal," Natalie said, "later after dinner do you

want to take some barometer readings with me?"

Hal shook his head, making sure he didn't feel too guilty. "Not tonight, Nats. I've got stuff to do."

Natalie frowned, and Hal caught the interest in his dad's gaze but chose to ignore that, too. He was planning a major step tonight. He glanced up to see his dad still watching him. *No,* he thought, *let's not talk about this. Really.*

Luckily, Laura Brandston chose that moment to barrel into the room, talking on her cell phone. She wore a business suit and only looked a little frazzled. Her hair was still neat and her eyes only a little red.

"Yeah, well you tell him if he's going to swim with the sharks," she said before anyone could say anything, "he's going to lose a little blood." Then she noticed her family staring at her. "Gotta go." She closed the cell phone. "I know. I'm late again. There's no excuse. I'm a rotten mother. I admit that. But in my heart, I know you'll find a way to forgive me, right?"

Tom looked at her blankly. "Uh-huh. And you are . . . ?"

Laura gave him a fake laugh. She stepped forward and took the straw from Randy's hand.

"No," Tom said, "I'm serious. Do you kids know who this lady is?"

"Very funny," Laura said. She sat down and groaned with relief. "Uhhh. You guys wouldn't believe it. Here I am twenty-four hours away from closing the biggest account of my life and they dump this

22

on my lap." She reached into a bag and pulled out a Mug Root Beer plush toy shaped like a barrel. "Thirteen thousand of these were just shipped to Beijing. It's supposed to say, 'The soft drink for a hard world . . .'" She pulled the string on the barrel. A fuzzy rabbit popped out of the barrel and made a barfing noise.

"Catchy," Hal said.

"I'm guessing there was a mix-up at the factory," Tom said.

Laura shook her head. "So . . . what did I miss?"

Randy looked up at her. "I stuck my whole fist in my mouth. Wanna see?" He opened his mouth wide and started shoving his fist inside.

Hal noticed both his parents were trying hard not to be alarmed.

"That's wonderful, honey," Laura replied, switching her gaze to Natalie. "How about you, Natalie? Eat any limbs?"

Laura's cell phone shrilled for attention. She gave Tom a helpless glance, obviously torn.

Tom pulled a dollar from his pocket and smoothed it out on the table. He pushed it toward her. "This dollar is yours if you let it ring."

She gave him an uneasy smile as she took the dollar. "Easiest buck I ever made. So how was everybody's day?"

Hal watched with interest. *Mom not answering a phone call? No way.* He pushed his plate away and ignored Natalie's accusing look.

The cell phone continued to ring. Finally Laura

couldn't take it anymore. She pushed the dollar back across the table to Tom as she picked up the phone. "I'll only be a second."

Tom nodded with a kind of sad smile, then picked the dollar up.

In his room, Hal ran his fingers over Claire's bracelet, working his courage up. The gold felt warm and heavy. He held the whale charm up and compared it to a picture of a whale in the encyclopedia. The caption read, "Nature's Gentle Giant."

They're big, Hal thought, looking at the world's largest mammal. *I can really understand what Claire sees in them. Big. Big and friendly.*

He shifted his attention back to the bracelet. Unable to resist the temptation any longer, he wrapped the bracelet around his own ankle. He wanted to make sure he could do it right when the time came to give it back to Claire. He didn't have a doubt that she would ask him to put it on for her.

"What . . . are . . . you . . . doing?"

Totally embarrassed, Hal tried to yank the bracelet off. But in his haste, his fingers turned clumsy. He couldn't get the bracelet off, and Natalie stood behind him, staring at it.

"Get out of here," Hal said in a strained voice. "I didn't say you could come in my room."

Natalie didn't budge, clearly enjoying having the upper hand. "Why are you wearing a girl's bracelet?"

"Get out of my room!" Hal tugged on the bracelet again. He felt bad about yelling at Natalie, but he felt

24

even worse about being discovered with Claire's bracelet wrapped around his ankle.

Natalie shot him a worried glance and left.

Hal gave a loud sigh and flopped back on the bed, wishing this whole thing with Claire would be easier. *But if it were, would it be worth doing?* Somehow he didn't think so.

Chapter
4

Natalie sat on her windowsill, wearing a coat against the chill. She looked out at the starlit sky. *It feels like winter, so where's the snow? Gotta have snow to have a real winter.*

She glanced down at the Mr. Science junior meteorology kit her dad had given her last year. She studied the barometer dial and recorded the reading in her notebook.

The door opened, and she glanced over to see her dad walking into her room.

"Hey, Nats." Tom crossed the room and sat down on the windowsill next to her. "Anything out there?"

"I think so," Natalie said. "It's getting colder out, and the needle moved a bit." She held up the barometer for inspection. The dial inside was divided into Clearing, Sunny, Cloudy, and Precipitation. The needle held steady between Sunny and Cloudy.

"So it has," her dad replied. "Well, maybe a little low pressure is heading this way."

"Bye, Mom," Hal called from the hallway. "I'm leaving."

The back door slammed, and Natalie glanced out the window in time to see Hal sprinting toward the street. He didn't even stop to wave good-bye. Natalie frowned. "Good."

Her dad raised his eyebrows at her.

"He's been acting all weird lately," Natalie said.

"Yeah, well, he's got a lot on his mind," her dad told her quietly. "You know, girls, umm . . . pretty much mostly girls, I think."

"Is that why he's wearing a girl's ankle bracelet?" Natalie asked innocently.

Tom straightened a little in surprise. "Could be. Could be. You see, Natalie, most boys Hal's age go through a stage where they like to experiment with things. . . . Are you sure it was an ankle bracelet?"

Natalie nodded.

"Well," Tom said, "it's all perfectly normal." He reached into his pocket and pulled out a small shaker bubble. "Your mom gave it to me when I started working at the station. It was supposed to be a good luck charm. Maybe it'll work better for you."

Natalie took the bubble from him, noticing the cabin under pine trees on a hill. She shook it, then held it up and studied the beautiful snowstorm now taking place in the liquid inside. "Cool. Thanks."

Her mom and Randy stepped into the doorway.

27

Randy's fist was in his mouth. "Could you guys help me here?" Laura asked. "It's stuck."

Tom stood. "Come on. I'll grab his arm and you hold his head."

Regretfully, Natalie followed her dad, leaving the barometer on the table. Even as she walked way, the needle plunged a little closer to Precipitation.

Dan's Diner was a favorite hangout for Syracuse high school students. Everybody who was anybody went there. Hal usually didn't go there much at all. But he knew Claire Bonner did.

Claire sat at the power booth in the corner with her friends, under the pictures of James Dean and Elvis. Marla, Fawn, and Paula, her usual companions, were with her. All of them were talking quietly.

There was no sign of Chuck Wheeler anywhere. Hal had checked the parking lot on the way in. No yellow convertible occupied any of the spaces out there. The weight of Claire's bracelet in his hand felt good. *Maybe just walking up and, saying, "Hello, I found your bracelet," wouldn't be so hard,* he tried to tell himself.

Hal was sitting with Lane and Bill at one of the lesser booths. "Don't tell me you don't see a pattern here," he told them. "The bracelet. The breakup. The fact that we're both big fans of whales."

Lane raised an eyebrow. "Whales."

"Yeah, whales." Hal opened his hand to show her the bracelet and the whale charm. "Nature's gentle giant. What's not to love?"

28

"Hal," Lane stated, "you're starting to scare me. If you want to go out with someone, go out with Patty Krone. For some reason she thinks you're cute."

Hal glanced over at the booth where Patty sat. Patty was cute, sweet, and average. He hadn't even thought of dating her. She sat there, talking with a friend, jiggling her leg in nervous excitement.

"Nah," Hal replied. "She's . . . a leg jiggler. I can't go out with a leg jiggler. Besides, this thing with me and Claire, it's destiny."

Lane looked at Bill, who had sucked all the air out of his glass so that it stuck to his face. "You catching any of this?" she asked.

Bill's voice was muffled by the glass, which wouldn't come off. "Uh-huh."

Lane looked at him doubtfully.

Hal straightened in his seat, not wanting to deal with any more sarcastic comments from Lane. "You want proof?" he asked. "Remember when I said I was waiting for the right moment to give Claire her bracelet back? Well, this is it."

She just looked at him, a half smile of amusement on her lips.

Hal acted more confident than he felt as he stood and put his empty milk shake glass down. Lane and Bill glanced at him in disbelief. *Why doesn't one of them try to stop me? That's what friends are for, to keep you from doing the really stupid things in life.*

But they didn't.

Hal took a deep breath and walked toward Claire.

He didn't know those few steps could last so long or be so hard. He held on to Claire's bracelet for luck and strength, feeling really confused.

Then he was at the table. Claire and her friends kept talking, never once looking up. He just knew they were going to hear his heart hammering inside his chest, or the way his breath rasped against the back of his throat, which had become dry and constricted.

They kept talking as if he wasn't even there.

Then he got it. He *wasn't* there. Not in their world. He turned away from the corner booth and walked to the front of the diner. He was through the front door before anyone could stop him. He waited out there, alone, until his heart slowed and he was sure no one was coming after him.

Dumb. Really dumb.

Later that night, sitting at his desk in his room. Hal held the bracelet up to the light. He was not going to do that again, he decided.

Lane is right. To people like Claire, people like me . . . well, we should know better.

He dropped the bracelet into an envelope and sighed. He addressed the envelope to Claire, then added a stamp and dropped it on the desk.

First thing tomorrow, he had decided on the walk home, *I'll drop the envelope in the mailbox and make my long overdue return to reality.*

In bed that night, Natalie played with the shaker bubble that contained a small house in a forest. Fake snow covered the ground inside the shaker bubble, but when she shook it vigorously, a blizzard formed, swirling and tumbling.

"I wish it was this easy," Natalie said, imagining what it would be like to be in a real snowstorm.

For a moment her imagination led her inside the bubble. Suddenly she was amid all the snow, running and sliding. She tilted her head up and stuck her tongue out.

"Natalie, what are you doing?"

Opening her eyes, Natalie suddenly realized her mom was standing in the doorway and she was lying there with her tongue stuck out. "Just catching some snowflakes."

Laura smiled. "They taste good?"

Natalie nodded.

Laura crossed the room and lowered the window shade. "You should really get to sleep, honey. It's getting late, and tomorrow's a school day."

Natalie sighed.

Laura kissed her cheek and turned the lights off. On the windowsill, the barometer needle dropped even closer to Precipitation.

That night at the television studio, preparing the weather forecast, Tom sat at his desk studying all the satellite photos on his computer. At least he *had* been studying them. Now he was blowing up a duck pool float he was expected to wear. He was dressed in a beach hat Tina Stillman had asked the wardrobe personnel to lay out for him. He wasn't happy about it.

"You're on in two minutes, Mr. Sunshine," Tina said.

Tom gave her a pained look as he blew the float up. "Oh, yeah? How come I'm the one blowing up the duck?"

"Just keep blowing," Tina said.

"That shouldn't be too hard," Tom said. He kept blowing, until he noticed what was taking place on the computer screen. "Whoa!" he exclaimed. He punched in numbers, checked other grids, and made notes. "That's not supposed to be there. Unless . . ." he paused, "the cold front I know about, but . . . that can't be right. Can it?"

He checked the numbers again.

On the telecast later, despite the tacky beachcomber getup and minus the duck float, Tom was all business. "Snow and lots of it, folks. This one almost caught us by surprise, but we're right on top of it."

Chapter 5

Natalie was the first one in the Brandston house to realize the snowstorm had blown into Syracuse. She'd gone to sleep with the shaker bubble in her hands and it had fallen to the floor. The noise woke her, and she slowly made her way to the window, opening the shade. The brightness streaming in from the window as the morning sun reflected off the blanket of snow almost blinded her.

After that, it didn't take her long to wake the rest of the house. They all heard her yell. "Snow!"

All of Syracuse was buried in mounds and mounds of pure white snow. It filled backyards and front yards; it covered cars, driveways, playgrounds and the golf course across the street. Business was halted. Before the morning traffic even got started, it ground to a halt.

Of course, all those folks who watched Chad Symmonz didn't have a clue.

Natalie, Randy, and Hal sat around the radio in Hal's bedroom, waiting anxiously. None of them had bothered to get dressed for school. They just sat there, breathless, fingers crossed.

"With last night's record snowfall grinding the Syracuse area to a halt," the DJ on the radio was saying, "the National Weather Service has issued a traveler's advisory for today."

Hal leaned closer to the radio, followed by Natalie and Randy.

"I'm sure you're wondering what's been closed," the DJ went on, "so let's get right to it."

All over Syracuse, plans were changing as people woke up to the fact that a blizzard had come overnight. Maybe it was more than plans, though. Maybe lives were out there changing. That was a lot of snow.

Kids and adults listened to the radio all across town. Breakfast came to a screeching halt as nervous mothers bit their nails down to nubs.

The kid dressed in the polar explorer outfit rubbed his lucky rabbit foot and paced in front of a wall map covered with pushpins from past explorations.

At home, Chet Felker poured himself a glass of orange juice and tossed it back.

At his home, Principal Weaver stopped brushing his teeth, dreading the coming announcement.

Wayne Alworth rocked on his knees in his bedroom, breathing into a paper bag.

"The following establishments are closed for today," the DJ announced. "Titan Tool and Dye, Cumberland Electric, Gearco, the Carousel Mall, the Health Barn . . ."

Hal listened intently. He didn't think any one of them was breathing.

"Tidy Boy Paints, Fromlin's Corduroy Shop," the DJ continued, "Sprocketland . . ."

"He's killing me, Hal," Natalie said through gritted teeth.

". . . the Rotary League Bowl-a-Thon, Saint Mary's Macramé and You Seminar, and finally, the weekly poker game at my house. That concludes the list of closings for today."

Hal couldn't believe it. He felt like he'd been hit by the high school's entire football defensive line.

Natalie slumped up against him, almost hard enough to knock him over. "No," she moaned. "They can't do that to us."

He put an arm around her shoulders, trying to comfort her. Natalie really looked forward to snow days.

"What a gyp," Randy said, looking totally bummed, too.

Then the DJ came back on, sounding reluctant. He was an adult, maybe even had kids of his own, so Hal guessed he could understand how the guy could be reluctant. "Oh, I forgot one," he said. "All schools are officially closed for a snow day."

Natalie cheered so loud in Hal's ear that he

thought he'd gone deaf. But he was cheering with her. In fact, he bet every kid in Syracuse was cheering right about then. The snow day they thought would never happen, the snow day every adult feared, had arrived.

Hal flopped backward onto the bed, trying to sort out all the options that were suddenly his for the taking. For a little while, for the space of a day, perhaps, he was invincible.

"Snow day. Snow day. Snow day. Snow day," Natalie sang. "I love the way it sounds."

Hal cupped his hands like a megaphone around his mouth. "Snow day!"

Natalie raced to the window to look out over the neighborhood. "Anything can happen."

Her words woke up the enthusiasm inside of Hal that he'd been truly lacking. At first the snow day had seemed more like a reprieve than anything else. Then he spotted the envelope addressed to Claire. "Yeah."

Even as the words left his lips, the sound of the most monstrous snowplow ever to dig Syracuse out of the grip of winter hammered through the house. It was a grinding, rumbling horror that every kid in town knew.

"Oh, no," Natalie said, gazing down at the street.

Hal didn't even have to look. He knew the monster snowplow from past snow days. Bigger than anything had a right to be, the snowplow was an unstoppable juggernaut. Across the front of the massive blade the driver had painted a picture of a woman lying down. "Darling Clementine" was written in script above the woman.

His name was Roger Stubblefield, but to most people he was known simply as . . .

"Snowplowman!" a kid out in the street screamed in terror.

Hal joined Natalie at the window in time to watch as kids ran for safety while the snowplow hurled the snow from the street. One kid dropped his sled, hesitated, then kept running. In the next instant, the sled shattered against Darling Clementine's mighty blade.

The driver sat in the enclosed cabin, its windows fogged over from the cold. All Hal could see of Snowplowman was the whites of his eyes and the glint of his teeth.

Over the years, he and his plow, Darling Clementine, had robbed kids of more snow days than anyone could count. The weather gods may giveth, but it was always Snowplowman who would taketh away.

"I really don't like him," Natalie said.

"He's not a fun guy," Hal agreed.

"He's got to be stopped. Today. What do you say, Hal? We said this was going to be the year, didn't we?"

"Nats . . ." Hal felt incredibly guilty.

"The prize: the legendary second snow day." She smiled slyly up at him. "Think of it, Hal. Two in a row. We've never had two in a row before!"

"Sorry," Hal said. "There's something I've got to do."

A sour look tightened Natalie's face. Then she spotted the envelope in his hand. Before he could stop her, she grabbed it.

"Claire Bonner?" she exploded. "Who's she?"

Hal felt really defensive. "Just this girl. You don't know her." He took the envelope back.

"Wait a second," Natalie said, understanding a lot more than any ten-year-old sister should. "You're gonna waste a snow day over some stupid girl?"

"Look, Nats, tomorrow everything goes back to normal. And when it does, I'll just be one of a million guys wishing that Claire Bonner was their girlfriend. But today maybe I can change all that. Like you said, Nats, on a day like today anything can happen."

Natalie's face fell, and she gave him a totally crushed look. "But we're a team."

"Yeah, and we always will be," Hal said, wishing he had something better to say. "But today I've just got to go solo. All right?"

Natalie looked at the floor. "I don't need you anyway." She left the room without another word.

Hal wanted to go after her, but he didn't know what he could say. He ripped the envelope open and dropped the ankle bracelet into his hand.

I didn't expect Natalie to understand. But what am I supposed to do? I've been given a second chance with Claire and I'm not going to blow it.

*   *   *

38

"There's no way I can stay home today," Hal pleaded, knowing he was trapped all the same.

"Well, then," Laura said, giving him fake understanding, "why don't we just leave Randy here all by himself?"

Randy stood by the refrigerator, filling his sneaker up with crushed ice from the automatic ice maker. Leaving him there by himself wasn't an option and Hal knew it.

Laura looked at Hal with a little more real understanding. "What do you want me to say, hon? I've been working on this account for two months." She closed her briefcase. "And I'm closing it *today*."

Hal shifted gears, turning his attention to his dad. "Why can't Dad stay? He doesn't go on until six o'clock."

"Sorry, pal," Tom answered. "I don't know if you heard."

For the first time Hal noticed that his dad had his favorite suit on. He couldn't remember when his dad had last worn it.

"Your father made Chad Symmonz eat it last night," Laura said.

Tom grinned. "Scooped him by ten minutes. Tina's got me doing live coverage all day. I think she's even going to let me wear pants."

"Would it make any difference to you guys if I told you that somewhere out there," Hal pointed out the window, "there's a girl who's in love with me, only she doesn't know it yet?"

Both parents seemed to give that some thought. "No," they said together.

Laura glanced at Hal sympathetically. "Hal, there'll be other snow days."

Hal opened his palm and stared down at the ankle bracelet. "Yeah," he said in a low voice, "you bet."

Chapter
6

Laura went out to the car and started going through her final checklist. "Okay. Briefcase, check. Commuter mug, check. Lucky troll doll . . ." She always reached out at that point to touch the fluorescent hair on the troll doll stuck to the dashboard. "Check. Look out Asian carbonated beverage market, here comes trouble."

She hit the garage door opener then, prepared to go out and bring the whole Pacific Rim soft drink market to its knees.

Only she wasn't going anywhere. As the garage door opened, Laura saw the giant wall of snow that blocked the way. She stared at it for perhaps a minute, then hit the garage door opener again, turned off the car, and went back into the house.

By the time she finished telling Tom and Hal what was going on, Hal was dressed and at the door.

Don't worry, Mom. There will be other workdays, he thought as he raced outside. He'd actually told her that, but she hadn't thought it was funny.

At that moment, Randy stepped around the corner with the vacuum cleaner, turned it on, and sucked Laura's skirt into the hose. Hal was gone before the wailing could begin.

But then again some people just don't see the beauty of a snow day, Hal thought as he passed people shoveling snow from their cars and driveways.

Hal laughed to himself and kept going, spotting Bruce Hebert ahead. The mailman struggled to get through the snow and stay on his feet.

"Neither rain nor sleet nor . . . what's the last one, Mr. Hebert?" Hal called out.

The mailman scowled, then ignored him.

Hal spotted Principal Weaver carrying a car broom. It was only a short distance to the car in his driveway, but he got caught in the crosshairs of what looked like a hundred snowballs that peppered him with white.

"Aaaah!" Principal Weaver screamed. "Stop it, you hoodlums!" He continued running toward the car, taking his keys out. "You want to play rough? I invented rough!" But he dropped the keys before he could use them. They disappeared in the waist-high snow.

Hal watched, amazed at the number of snowballs in the air.

Principal Weaver turned and tried to make it back to the house, but the snowballs cut him off. He turned, sprinted across the yard, and ran down the street.

Hal went on, cutting across the street to the snow-covered golf course. Only a short distance across, he spotted the polar explorer kid, who squared off against him.

The kid was all bundled up in a fur-lined parka, a long scarf, and ski goggles.

Hal recognized him at once; at least, he knew what the kid was supposed to be. He was a polar explorer, off to discover a pole. Hal and Nats had been polar explorers on snow days in the past.

The kid piled a thermos and some cheese-and-cracker snacks onto his sledding saucer. One end of a rope was attached to the saucer and the other end was attached to the collar of a big fat beagle.

"Well," the kid said, turning to Hal, "if it isn't Commander Scott. I must admit I'm surprised to see you. Thought you would have turned tail by now."

Hal looked at him, trying to figure out what planet he'd come from. "You did?"

"Don't play dumb with me, Scott. If you think you can beat me to the pole, well you're even more daft than you look!" He turned his attention to the beagle. "Mush, Roscoe! Mush! To the top of the world!"

But the pooch had other ideas. He snurfled once, then put his head on his forepaws and continued to lie there. The polar explorer didn't let that hold him back, though. He took hold of the beagle's collar and led him forward.

Hal couldn't do anything but shake his head and watch them walk away. Then he got ambushed from behind. Somebody jumped onto his back, staggering him. He barely kept his balance.

"You have the reflexes of a dead cow," Lane told him.

"And yet it would seem that it is I who have you in the oxygen-depriving sleeper hold." Hal dropped her off his back and started wrestling. In a short time he had her pinned in the snow.

"Okay . . . okay," she said, "you win!"

Hal released her and flopped down beside her. She moved her arms and legs, making a snow angel.

"I wonder if in Hawaii, instead of snow days, they have lava days," Lane said.

Hal laughed. "In Los Angeles I heard they get off school on bad hair days."

"I heard that."

Hal pushed up from the ground and turned around to look at the snow angel Lane had made. It looked pretty good.

"You know," Lane said, still lying there, "the problem with snow angels is that you can never make an absolutely perfect one. There's always the handprint you make when you climb out."

He bent down and picked her up. "Not always."

Lane turned to look at the snow angel she'd left behind. "It's perfect."

"It sure is," Hal agreed.

He turned and dropped her into a nearby snow-bank, grinning broadly.

Surprisingly, Lane didn't get upset at all. "Hey, you know what we can do today?" she asked. "Start an *avalanche!*"

Testing the water, Hal pulled out Claire's ankle bracelet. "I've got a bracelet to return."

Disbelief filled Lane's face. She slumped back into the snow. "No. No, no. No, no, no, no, no."

Hal didn't let her lack of enthusiasm get to him. "This snow day happened for a reason. It's giving me a second chance with Claire."

Lane groaned. "What do you think she's going to do? Hug you to her chest, lick your ear, and call you Bunky?"

"Okay. Fine," he told her. "Maybe you don't believe in true love, but I do."

She scowled at him, one of the best scowls he'd ever seen. "Is that what you think this is? God, you're dumb. Hal, love isn't about fate and magic bracelets and all that other junk. It's about finding someone you can stand to be around for ten minutes at a time."

"You're a real romantic, you know that?" he asked.

Lane shrugged and sighed, her breath pluming out in icy gray vapor that was torn to pieces by the wind. "This is going to end in flames."

Hal looked out over the snow. "Come on, Lane, have a little faith. It *is* a snow day." He couldn't help grinning.

Natalie retreated to the snow fort she'd built into the side of a snowbank. She dragged an old beanbag chair through the snow, carefully avoiding the orange extension cord that snaked through the snow, and stuffed the chair through the narrow doorway.

Wayne and Chet were both there when she crawled inside. They sat watching the color television in the middle of the floor. Natalie hadn't hooked up the cable, but the local channel reception was good.

Instead of doing the things she'd told them to do, both boys were playing a video game. The sounds of the game filled the snow fort.

"What do you think you're doing?" Natalie demanded.

"Turbo-Blast Indy 500," Wayne replied, eating snow. His eyes never left the screen and he cheered when Chet mowed down another victim. "It's like the real Indy except you get points for hitting people."

"I thought I told you guys to lay down the shag."

"We will," Chet promised. He wore a snazzy motorcycle helmet. He looked away from her stern glance. "I though this was supposed to be a day off."

Natalie glanced around the snow fort, noticing something was missing. Then she remembered what it was. "Wayne, what happened to the snow sofa?"

Wayne looked guilty. "I ate it."

"Wayno," Natalie said, "I'd be careful about eating too much of that stuff."

"With all those layers you're wearing," Chet put in, "if you have to go to the bathroom, I dunno, it could be close."

And Wayne was wrapped up in layers like some kind of Egyptian winter mummy. But he just waved them off, watching as Natalie took an action figure from her coat pocket. "All right, you brought Meltar." He took the doll and did his best Meltar impression. " 'I am the Questmaster.' So where's his ever faithful sidekick, Fangor?"

Natalie frowned sourly. "Chasing some girl."

Wayne and Chet looked at her and started to say something.

"Don't even ask," Natalie warned.

Both of them took it to heart.

"So what's our quest, mighty Questmaster?" Wayne asked.

Natalie shrugged as innocently as she could. "You know what Meltar says: 'Listen to the wind.' "

And a loud rumbling rattled into the snow fort, causing a small storm of falling snow.

Wayne looked around in pure terror. "That's not the wind."

Chet peered through the makeshift periscope and confirmed their worst fears. "Snowplowman."

Chapter 7

Nobody knew where the city got the snowplow. Somebody suggested maybe it came from Texas. They made everything big down there, and this snowplow was as big as a locomotive engine. It clanked and rumbled down the street, spreading terror throughout the neighborhood. Kids crowded the curb and watched the big monster coming, not believing what was happening.

The driver sat in his cabin on top of the big machine. Natalie saw that evil grin all the way down the block. The snowplow blade caught the white snow up and turned it, clumping it instantly and giving it that dirty cottony look.

The driver glowered at the world from his high seat. He was forty-something and just this side of gnarly. He was taller and bigger than any man any kid had ever seen outside of the World Wrestling

Federation. As usual, he wore a long overcoat, cowboy boots, and fingerless gloves. His hair was cropped short, almost to the scalp. He looked like one of those old-time gunslingers.

The snowplow cut through the newly fallen snow like it was nothing, blazing a path that promised free passage for normal traffic by morning. Most kids scattered as the snowplow neared them because it turned the snow in huge waves a surfer could appreciate. One little kid dressed in a snowsuit and sucking on an icicle didn't get out of the way in time and went down under an avalanche of snow.

Stubblefield looked in his rearview mirror and laughed.

Some people said Stubblefield hated snow days because he never had one. Stories had even been told that his family was so poor he had to shovel driveways to help put food on the table. Sometimes driveways weren't enough. There were stories that Stubblefield used to clear major highways with a shovel all by himself.

As he grew, so did his hatred. Legend had it that the chains on his wheels were made from the braces of kids who didn't get out of his way.

Natalie watched as the snowplow's massive chains tore into the snow. Inside the cab, Stubblefield poured himself a cup of coffee from the grimy giant Thermos he kept. And he did it without stopping or slowing Clementine, and without spilling a drop. He also poured some coffee into a cup near the small bird that rode in the cab with him. When he whistled a sweetly haunting bird song, the bird flew over to the cup, perched, and took a sip.

People said the only thing Snowplowman really cared about was his bird, Trudy.

The neighborhood kids watched as Stubblefield plowed up the street, building huge mounds of dirty snow on either side. In seconds he was stripping them of their snow day.

Natalie glared at the snowplow and Stubblefield as machine and man got closer. She felt really afraid, but she made herself stay put.

Wayne shook his head. "I don't know about this. Couldn't we just go back and make a snowman?"

Natalie couldn't give the idea up. "No way. This is the year Hal and I said we were going to take him down."

"Yeah well," Wayne said with relief, "Hal's not here."

Natalie glared him down. "Snowball," she ordered. "Now." She reached back, waiting.

Grinning, Chet took a snowball from the cooler they'd prepared. "What do you need? I got your standard slushball, always dependable, or the ever popular moonball." He took out a snowball with a hole in the center and held it up to his eye. "The last thing he sees before it hits him is you mooning him. I've got the jelly-filled snow nut, and this one." He held up a yellow snowball in a plastic bag. "It speaks for itself."

Natalie wrinkled her nose at the yellow snowball. "Give me the snow nut."

Wayne's eyes got big, not believing what he was seeing. "Man, oh, Manitoba. Dr. Kleinmarker says with a nervous condition like mine any stressful situation could turn my bladder into a ticking time bomb." Then the look of disbelief got even bigger. "You see? Ah, man, I gotta whiz." He turned and sprinted off, heading toward the snow fort.

Stubblefield and Clementine kept coming closer, ripping away the snow day and all it had to offer.

"It's now or never," Chet told Natalie.

Natalie smiled, one of those smiles she always shared with Meltar when they had Dr. Freon or another baddie on the run. "I'll go with . . . *now!*" She wound up and threw the snowball with everything she had.

The snowball sailed straight as a bullet, homing in like a guided missile. It soared through the snow-plow's window and slammed into Stubblefield's head.

The snowball smeared across Stubblefield's face, temporarily blinding him. He lost control of Clementine and sideswiped a car, rocking it off its wheels on that side. A few seconds later, the snowplow rolled to a sudden stop against a tree. The engine clanked, sputtered, and died.

Silence descended over the neighborhood. No one had ever seen Stubblefield or Clementine motionless when there were streets to be cleared. The neighborhood kids started creeping closer.

"That was easy," Chet whispered, as if witnessing a miracle.

"We stopped him," Natalie said. "We did it. Do you know what this means?"

"The legendary second snow day," Chet said in awe.

But Stubblefield wasn't down for the count yet. He brushed the snow out of his eyes and turned his head, spotting Natalie and Chet almost at once. He turned the engine over and it caught, sending a blast of black diesel smoke billowing into the air.

Chet and Natalie spotted Stubblefield too. "Run!" they shouted.

Stubblefield gunned Clementine's engine before they could even turn to run. The snowplow shivered and shook like a wet dog, then cut across the street and came roaring at them.

"Run!" Natalie yelled.

They ran as if they were competing at the Olympics, heading toward the fort in the backyard. They passed Wayne who was still answering the call of nature.

"Put some oomph into it, Wayno," Chet called out.

Wayne gazed over his shoulder, torn between two necessities. "No! Don't leave me here! I don't want to die with my pants off!" He barely managed to pull himself together in time, pants down around his ankles, to get a running start ahead of the behemoth barreling down on them.

Stubblefield lowered the plow blade more, skimming only inches above the ground. He spoke to the bird. "If you can't hunt with the big dogs, you better sit on the porch with the pups."

Natalie led the retreat. She dropped into the tunnel that led to their fort. But Stubblefield wasn't stopping. They slid down the slope at the end of the backyard that led out onto the cross street.

Clementine didn't pause. Stubblefield put his foot down harder on the accelerator, rocketing across the backyard. If it hadn't been for the snow, the oversize tires would have shredded the lawn. He rolled into the snow fort, colliding with it hard enough to shiver just for an instant.

The big snow tires rolled over the beanbag chair and burst it like a balloon, shooting multicolored beans in all directions. The television shattered into glass and plastic confetti. Only debris remained of the snow fort when Clementine powered through. Stubblefield didn't even hesitate at the slope. The snowplow's big tires ate up the distance and he expertly used the big blade itself to control his skid back onto the cross street.

"Natalie!" Chet said, leading the charge down the street. "Let's go! This freak show means business!"

"So do we," Natalie said.

Stubblefield kept on rolling, stripping snow day from the streets of Syracuse. But he had made an enemy, one who'd defeated villains who'd threatened galaxies. Then again, Natalie and Meltar had never taken on anyone like Snowplowman.

Chapter 8

Laura scanned the kitchen hopefully. She'd changed the dining room into a makeshift home office for the day. Her laptop was on the dining table, hooked into the fax and scanner peripherals, the phone line, the modem, and the printer. She'd even hooked in the digital video camera that would allow her to be seen over Internet video phone hookups.

The perfect makeshift corporate environment had been successfully installed. However, there was still a loose cannon: Randy.

On the computer screen, Laura's personal assistant's video image showed digitized doubt. Nona was in her mid-twenties and close to panic. "I can't believe this. The office is closed down and you make me come to work. I had to walk the whole way." She propped her bare feet up on her desk at the office. They were still blue. "Look at my toes. They're frozen." She flicked them with a finger and the tiny dulled *thunk* echoed over the Internet connection. "Like Tater Tots."

"What was I supposed to do, Nona?" Laura asked. "I'm completely snowed in."

"Yeah, well, I want you to apologize to my toes. Go ahead. They're waiting."

"Toes," Laura said, "I am truly sorry for what I put you through. How's that? Better?"

"No. Everybody else is taking the day off. Why can't we?"

"Because we've been working too long and too hard to let a little snow get in the way of a potential forty-two percent global market share."

Nona pulled the string on the barrel of the new toy they were marketing. The rabbit popped out and made a barfing noise.

"Come on," Laura coaxed. "It'll be fun. Now the first thing I'll need is the quarterly earnings report."

Nona was distracted by something behind Laura. "The first thing you'll need is a stun gun for your kid."

Catching the clue, Laura turned in her office chair and spotted Randy wearing his lunchbox like a helmet and pounding his head into the door.

"Let me call you back," Laura said. She punched off the connection and ran over to her son. "Randy, that's no way to treat your head."

"I wanna go outside." Randy crossed his arms over his chest. "Mrs. Huffner lets us go outside at school."

"I know she does, honey," Laura explained. "But remember what Mommy told you? Once I get my work done then we can go out. Okay?" She patted him on the head, then returned to the table.

Randy followed her and climbed into her lap. "Tell me a story."

Laura nodded and kind of went along with it. "All right. Once upon a time, in a land far, far away, there lived a handsome little prince—"

"Mrs. Huffner tells us a story about a pokey little puppy."

Laura took a deep breath, already getting sick of how perfect Mrs. Huffner seemed to be. "I see. Well, Mommy doesn't know that story. But can Mrs. Huffner do this?" She put her fingers behind her head like donkey ears and hee-hawed loudly.

"Mrs. Huffner brings in a real donkey," Randy replied.

Laura felt beaten for a moment. "Uh-huh. Well, did Mrs. Huffner give you that new paint set you wanted for your birthday a whole week early?"

"Yeah!" Randy squealed. He hopped out of her lap and ran toward the playroom.

Laura breathed a sigh of relief and turned back to the papers Nona was already e-mailing to her. "Take that, Mrs. Huffner."

Lane and Hal strode through the winter wonderland that had bombed mostly unprepared Syracuse overnight. A lot of folks were still out, milling around their homes and wondering where all the snow had come from.

Their attention, however, was totally drawn to Principal Weaver as he came running toward them. The principal was totally panicked. When he saw them, he stopped running and tried to act nonchalant.

"Hey, kids," he said. "Enjoying your day off? I know I sure am."

A couple dozen snowballs suddenly exploded against the principal.

Principal Weaver flicked snow off his clothing. "Ha-ha. Those scamps! Well, I'd best be going." He started walking away, then broke into a run as more snowballs hit all around him.

Hal lost it and was quickly joined by Lane. Then he saw something that was potentially not so funny.

Seeing the Channel 6 Action Weather van at the top of Slupperton Hill surprised him. He knew that his dad was going to be out doing live coverage of the storm's effects, but he didn't know they were going to be doing it so close to home.

Or so close to Claire's house.

A crew was putting up lights so they could go live.

Lane put a hand over her eyes, shielding them from the harsh glare of the sun. "Is that your dad over there?"

Hal looked in the direction she pointed, recognizing his dad almost immediately in spite of the outfit he knew Ms. Stillman must have told him to wear.

He was dressed as Frosty the snowman, and he looked ridiculous.

"Yeah," Hal replied. "He must be here to cover my big moment with Claire. It's good for ratings. People love that kind of stuff."

Lane gave him a fake smile with so much sugary sweetness that he should have dropped into a diabetic coma then and there. "Especially the part where the ex-boyfriend returns and rearranges your face."

Hal had to admit that brought him back to earth for just a minute, even though it was snow day. He put on a brave front anyway. "Chuck? Pffft. If he shows up, he's just going to have to deal with it. Today she's all mine." And he felt pretty confident about that because the snow day magic was in the air.

The confidence, however, only lasted till he turned the corner near the Channel 6 Action Weather van and walked down Claire's street. What he saw in Claire's front yard froze him in his tracks.

Chapter 9

Hal swallowed hard in disbelief as he looked at Claire's front yard.

Over two dozen guys were hanging around there. They wore leather jackets, letter jackets, or trench coats over suit jackets. One guy was reciting bad poetry through a bullhorn. A guy with an oboe was dueling with a guy on a keyboard guitar. Another guy carried an enormous cactus in a pot. Still another guy was trying to spray paint a message in the snow.

"It's like Claire-stock," Lane said, smiling.

Hal walked over to his friend Bill, who was carrying a big bouquet of flowers and rehearsing his lines to himself. "Hey Claire. It's Bill. Bill Korn. Bill Korn, from the swim team. You know, the nosebleed guy?"

"Bill, what's going on here?" Hal asked accusingly.

"I'll give you three guesses and the first two don't count." Bill glanced away when Hal glared at him. "Word gets around, dude. It's not like you're the only one who heard they broke up. Some of these guys came all the way from Rochester."

Hal blinked again and turned away from Bill, staring out over the mass of guys gathered in front of her house. It looked as if every guy in Syracuse had shown up.

Inside the house, Claire was just getting her morning started, stumbling around and dressing to meet the day. She was one of those people who liked to start their snow days with a little more sleep. She stretched and yawned, then looked out the window.

A boy was standing on her balcony.

Claire screamed, totally losing it for just a second. The boy fell into a deep snowbank.

All the guys out there started clapping and yelling, waving to get her attention as they shouted out her name.

Blown away by the sudden attention, Claire closed the curtains and walked back to bed, hoping maybe she was just having some kind of bad dream.

Lane's giggling got the best of Hal. He shook his head in disgust. This was *not* what snow days were supposed to be about.

Hal glared at Bill and his fistful of flowers. "Bill, I don't exactly know how to put this, but seriously, what chance do you really have with someone like Claire?"

"Um, let me see. About as much chance as you," Bill replied.

That made Lane start cackling with glee again, which made the skin across the back of Hal's neck burn. He tried to think of a put-down that would have left Bill in flames, but before he could, a loud engine roar screamed across the street.

In a roiling cloud of powdery snow, Chuck Wheeler arrived, hanging on to a souped-up snowmobile. He gunned the snowmobile's engine and threaded through all the guys scattered across the lawn to Claire's house. "You've got to be kidding me," Chuck moaned. "You've *got* to be *kidding* me."

Hal totally understood how Chuck felt.

"All right, you zips, time to go home!" Chuck shouted. "Contrary to recent reports, me and the lady Claire are still very much in love. You got that, Korn?" He grabbed the flowers out of Bill's hands, then glared around at the rest of them, daring anyone to argue with him. "Now get out of my sight before you all get free passes to the Chuck Wheeler House of Pain."

"Not to be confused with the Chuck Wheeler Pain Hut," Lane whispered sarcastically.

Slowly and reluctantly, the guys moved back from Claire's yard.

Chuck gunned the snowmobile's engine and slid up under Claire's window. "Claire bear, it's me. Let me up. We gotta talk."

Instead, the television newscast from inside suddenly blared. The Channel 6 Action News theme played, then Phyllis's voice came on: "Stay with us, won't you? We'll be right back with a live Channel Six Accu-weather update right after this."

"Claire!" Chuck bellowed. "I'm begging you!"

Claire appeared and opened the window. "Sorry, Chuck. I can't. There's a live Channel Six Accu-weather update that I really don't want to miss."

"The only update I care about is the one that says we're getting back together. Please. If our three years mean anything to you, just give me one little minute."

"All right," Claire called down. "But only a minute."

Chuck leaped off the snowmobile and jogged toward the front door.

Hal watched it, saw it happen, and still couldn't believe it. His stomach did flip-flops. *Where is the snow day magic I am so due?*

"Cheer up. At least she watches your dad's station." Lane glanced at him, looking relieved.

An idea formed inside Hal's head. "Yes, she does," he stated slowly.

"It's not fair," Tom said into the microphone near his mouth. It was hard for him to talk while the wardrobe manager was finishing up his Frosty the Weatherman outfit. The bulky white sweater made him look misshapen, and the black buttons were as big as chocolate chip cookies. In addition to the stovepipe hat, he had a long scarf and a corncob pipe.

"You said you wanted to wear pants," Tina

replied over the earphone. She was back at the studio, watching over the remote camera. "You're wearing pants."

Tom sighed and glanced over his shoulder, upsetting the wardrobe manager. He watched the kids speeding down Slupperton Hill on sleds, toboggans, and saucers. The snow reinforced everything he had to say to his producer. "Tina, people don't want this Frosty the Weatherman stuff. They don't. I've seen it in their eyes. They want real weather from the only guy in town who knows what he's doing."

"Actually, Tom," Tina said, "research shows they want someone who can juggle fire and make cool sound effect noises."

"No. You're wrong. People will find out who predicted that storm first." Tom tried hard to convince himself. "The truth will become known. And when it does . . . watch out, Chad Symmonz."

Across town in the Channel 10 editing room, Chad Symmonz, his editor, and his producer watched a monitor that rolled footage of a howling rainstorm.

"Who was there when El Niño went el loco?" the TV announcer asked.

The scene cut to a crossing guard guiding kids across the street. He leaned out and talked to the camera. "Chad Symmonz!"

Footage of a tornado scrolled across the screen. "Who was there when a killer tornado devastated downtown?"

A father teaching his kid to ride a bike glanced up and talked to the camera. "Chad Symmonz!"

Then footage of the snowstorm that had buried Syracuse last night filled the screen. "And who was there last night when the blizzard of the century came knocking on our door?"

The scene cut again. Chad tore a printout from a computer. "Why, Chad Symmonz, of course. Whenever there's weather that affects our area, you can bet your boots I'll be there first." He gave the audience a thumbs-up and went back to his charts.

In the editing room, Chad watched the latest footage of himself fade from the screen. He nodded to the editor and producer seated in front of him. " 'You can bet your boots' . . . do you guys like that? My masseuse came up with it. Thought it made me sound earthy."

The editor scratched his head and looked at the producer. "Um, Chad . . . wasn't Brandston at Channel Six the first guy to call the storm?"

Chad glanced at the man. "How about this line, Mel? 'You can bet your boots you'll be fired if you ever second-guess me again.' "

The producer hunkered down and didn't look at Chad.

Chad grinned and walked away.

"Just kill me now," Tom muttered as he waited for his cue.

One of the crew counted him down with a fistful

of fingers, going from five to zero. Then he pointed, letting Tom know he was on.

"Let it snow, let it snow, let it snow!" Tom Brandston said on the television broadcast. "That's what kids all over central New York are saying today as last night's record snowfall turned their world into a winter wonderland!"

Laura looked over from the computer monitor, seeing the costume her husband had on. She poured herself a cup of coffee and shook her head sympathetically. "Oh, honey . . ."

Claire watched the weather telecast, really working on ignoring Chuck.

Chuck was working on being chummy. He sat on the sofa in the living room, watching the Channel 6 Action Weather update. Claire sat on the other end of the sofa, trying to figure out some way to really clue Chuck in to the whole situation. She watched as Tom Brandston walked over to the toboggan run where all the kids were playing.

"I'm here at Slupperton Hill or, as the kids who've shown up here today like to call it, Suicide Hill," Tom Brandston said.

Chuck wasn't making it easy to ignore him. "This isn't so bad, is it?" he asked. "You and me. Sitting here. Talking."

Claire just shook her head. "Chuck, what part of 'We broke up' don't you understand?"

"Every part of it," Chuck replied. "What happened last night was last night. Today . . . today is a day to go skating. It's the perfect way to show the gang we're back together."

"We're not back together."

"Yeah, well not technically."

Claire had to laugh. She'd never seen anybody act so dense in her life. Chuck never even noticed.

"I'm starving," Chuck told her. "Do you have anything to eat?"

She pointed to the kitchen. When he left, she turned her attention back to the television where Tom Brandston was continuing with his report. Some kids volunteered to give Frosty the Weatherman a toboggan ride down Slupperton Hill.

Tom climbed onto a toboggan. Kids flanked him, snickering evilly. "And what better way to say, 'Yeah, winter!' than with a good old-fashioned toboggan ride. If I could ask my helpers here to give me a little push . . ." Tom held his microphone out to one of the crew.

Without warning, the kids *shoved* the weatherman down Slupperton Hill instead of letting him slide on his own. Some of them ran alongside the toboggan and kept pushing till it was going so fast they couldn't keep up. When the toboggan reached that speed, they dropped in their tracks.

"I said a *little* push! Aaaahhhhh!" And Tom zoomed down the hill. He continued gathering speed, not even bothering with the script, hanging on for dear life. The cameraman followed Tom's course as he flew down the hill.

For a short time, the toboggan stayed on course. Then it hit a jump and Tom was airborne. He started screaming and didn't stop until he smashed into a snowbank that collapsed down over him.

When he looked up, a billboard with the smiling face of Chad Symmonz stared down at him.

Just then a boy Claire vaguely remembered stepped onto the screen. He held Tom's microphone in one hand. "That was Tom Brandston on weather," he said. "Thanks, Tom. Next up, a special message for Claire Bonner."

Back at the station, Tina Stillman sat bolt upright in her chair. "What is this? Frank!" She yelled into the mike hanging by her mouth. "Pan off him! Pan off him, Frank!"

Unfortunately, Frank was busy helping Tom in the background. The camera kept rolling.

Chapter
10

"Claire, I know you're watching. My name's Hal. You don't know me, but I know you."

Claire watched, totally hypnotized. She couldn't believe it. She stared at the boy with the microphone, wondering where she'd seen him before, wondering what he was going to say next.

On her television screen, Hal continued. "Like I know that your favorite gum is Watermelon Bubblicious, that you can't go a day without diving, and that your eyes are browner . . . browner than brown is supposed to be. I also know that yesterday, America's Dream Team broke up."

Chuck emptied a box of cereal into a mixing bowl until the toy prize fell out. He picked it up from the bowl, totally happy. "Choice."

*   *   *

In the living room, Claire watched Hal.

The boy on television moved closer to the camera. "Personally, I think it was the right move. So today if you're wondering what to do next, I say you try something new. Me. Yeah, me. It's a snow day, Claire. Anything can happen."

A "Please Stand By" graphic slid into place on the screen as the studio cut the transmission.

While Claire sat there, trying to figure out if she'd ever seen the guy before, Chuck returned from the kitchen and sat down beside her.

"Claire," he said, "I know you're mad at me, but I've been doing a lot of soul-searching. And hopefully this will change your mind." He held up a miniature hypno-disc and twirled it in front of her face.

Claire recognized the toy as the one from the cereal box, but she didn't say anything. First there was the guy on the television, now Chuck was acting weird. The snow day was getting way beyond her control.

Chuck pitched his voice low, like a hypnotist, talking slowly and using a really bad accent. "You are not mad anymore. Even though your boyfriend can be a major load sometimes, you can't resist him. Now, when I blow in your ear, you will put on your long underwear and go skating with him." He blew in her ear.

Despite the tension between them, Claire smiled. This was more like the old Chuck, more like the guy she'd fallen in love with.

"So what do you say?"

She refused to answer.

He twirled his little hypno-disc. "You are not mad anymore. . . ."

Claire couldn't help herself, won over by his antics. "All right. All right. I'll go."

"You know, Hal, when I was your age, I'd get a girl to notice me by wearing cologne." Tom leaned against the Channel 6 news van and held a handful of snow against the knot on his head. Hal and Lane stood nearby.

Hal ducked his head and apologized. "I'm sorry, Dad. But this girl, she's so . . . I mean, she just, just . . ."

"Gets you all wiggly?" his dad asked. "Got it. You do what you have to do and don't worry about me. We meteorologists are trained to deal with the unpredictable."

One of the technicians from the on-site crew walked over to Tom. "Uh, Tom. You might want to take a look at this. We were taping the Channel Ten feed and, um . . ." Obviously, the man didn't want to go on.

Hal stood beside his father as they watched Chad Symmonz taking credit for predicting the snowstorm first. Then Tom stalked off and started throwing snowballs at the billboard with Chad Symmonz's photo on it. "Liar! Liar! Liar!"

Hal figured maybe it was a good time to move on. He went over to join Lane, who was watching his dad. "So," he said, "how was I?"

"Remember in sixth grade when you wore those rainbow suspenders all the time because you thought they were cool?" she asked, showing no mercy at all. "Kind of like that."

Hal tried not to worry. "I know what I'm doing, okay?"

"Then enlighten me," she replied, pointing off into the distance. "How does *that* work into your plans?"

Hal followed her pointing finger back toward Claire's yard, his heart already sinking. Claire was outside her house now, climbing onto Chuck's souped-up snowmobile. Suddenly, snow day or no snow day, Hal felt lousy.

Maybe Lane felt bad for him, because she didn't try to hit him when he was down, standing there flat-footed with his mouth open. That kind of made him feel even worse because there was usually no pity between Lane and him.

"What did you expect, Hal?" she asked softly. "They always get back together. That's what they do. I know you think today is supposed to be all supermagical, but to them it's just another stupid Tuesday."

At the moment Hal felt like he didn't have a reason to take another breath. Everything just kind of drained out of him as he watched Chuck fire up the snowmobile and shoot forward, curving around toward them.

Hal didn't think Chuck even saw him. But Claire did. For just an instant, at least. She looked right at

71

him while she was holding on to Chuck. *Right at me.* And she smiled. Not one of those I-know-I'm-cute smiles, but a smile that let Hal know she'd seen him and heard him and, most important, understood him.

"Stupid Tuesday, huh," he told Lane. Suddenly he felt ten feet tall and bulletproof again. Like Fangor, companion to Meltar, off on another crusade to save some poor, evil-ridden galaxy.

Chuck's snowmobile drove out of sight. He and Claire were gone in seconds. But the snowmobile's tracked drive belt left deep ruts in the snow, blazing the trail.

Hal couldn't help himself; he started off at once, clumping through the snow. After a long moment he heard Lane's snow boots crunching along behind him. *This year, Lane, I'm going to teach you to really believe in the magic of snow days.*

Natalie upended the ketchup bottle and splattered Wayne. "Awww, man. Why do I have to be the decoy?" Wayne asked. "I'm the one who got the ketchup."

Chet placed a broken sled near Wayne's feet. "Shh. If you don't play dead, you're gonna *be* dead."

"Here he comes," Natalie said.

The horrendous noise of the snowplow echoed along the street long before Darling Clementine swung around the corner. Natalie and Chet took up positions behind a snow-buried car.

"Next time," Wayne told them, "bring your own ketchup! This better not stain my coat."

"Snow and lots of it, folks. This one almost caught us by surprise, but we're right on top of it."

"Hal, love isn't about fate and magic bracelets and all that other junk. It's about finding someone you can stand to be around for ten minutes at a time."

"Snowplowman."

"I don't know about this. Couldn't we just go back and make a snowman?"

"Hey Claire. It's Bill. Bill Korn. Bill Korn, from the swim team. You know, the nosebleed guy?"

"Word gets around, dude. It's not like you're the only one who heard they broke up. Some of these guys came all the way from Rochester."

"I said a *little* push! AAAAHHHH!!!"

"Chuck, who am I as a person? We've been dating for three years. What do you really know about me?"

"Sorry I'm late, but I had to pick up a friend."

"You know when you're making a snow angel and you want to make it perfect but you can't because you always leave a handprint when you climb out? Well, with Hal, there's no handprint."

"He's off building some kind of shrine to the Lady Claire."

"Hi, I'm Greg. I'll be hurting you this afternoon."

"That's right. Old Jack Frost here, taking you on a tour of this year's Winter Jamboree."

"Stop it, Randy! It's very, very important that mommy finds her phone!"

"I'm here on West Burlington Street—or should I say Burrrrrlington Street, ha-ha—where it's good to see that this record snowfall hasn't stopped some of my weather fans from turning out."

"Listen to the wind!"

"Nooo!! You can't take Clementine!"

They didn't have long to wait to spring their trap.

The noisy rumble of Darling Clementine scraping snow from the streets came closer and closer. The black smoke roiling from her quivering stacks came around the corner. Huge piles of snow crashed and broke across the blade, obediently forming snow hills on the side of the street. It rumbled straight for Wayne.

Wayne flinched a little, but who could blame him? Stubblefield didn't care about anybody, except Trudy the parakeet, and that was what Natalie was planning on.

Even across half the street, Natalie saw Wayne swallow hard.

"O my darling Clementine!" Stubblefield sang between eating fries left over from lunch. "She was lost and gone forever, dreadful sorrow, Clementine." Spotting Wayne in the middle of the road, he hit the brakes quickly. Darling Clementine came to a stop twenty yards from Wayne.

Snowplowman glanced in all directions, but there was nobody but Wayne to see. So he popped open the cab door and stepped down to the street. He walked slowly toward Wayne.

Chapter
11

Already in motion, knowing they were only going to get one chance, Natalie and Chet crept out from behind the snow-covered car where they had hidden. They slipped around behind Stubblefield, silent as ghosts, knowing they were on the edge of becoming real ghosts if Snowplowman caught them.

Stubblefield was still holding a box of french fries in one semi-gloved hand. It didn't seem to matter to him that Wayne looked all blood-covered. He came to a stop by Wayne and prodded him with the pointed toe of his boot.

To his credit, Wayne remained corpse-like.

"Stay here," Natalie whispered to Chet as she pushed herself up into the snowplow's cab. "I'm going for the keys."

Chet nodded and stepped around in front of Darling Clementine. He took out the bottle of green fingerpaint Natalie had borrowed from Randy's paint set and got to work defacing the image on the snowplow blade.

Natalie pulled herself up onto the door landing, then worked hard to quietly open the massive door. Once she was inside, she couldn't help but kind of freeze up. She hadn't known what to expect inside the truck. She'd been expecting creepy and grimy, but she hadn't expected the hairless doll's head wedged onto the end of the gearshift. That locked her up for a minute. There was also a copy of *How to Write a Screenplay in 21 Days*.

She glanced out the window and watched Stubblefield squat next to Wayne. Knowing they were almost out of time, she reached for the keys. Before she could get them, Trudy the parakeet exploded into action, squawking and beating her wings against Natalie's face.

Natalie nearly lost it. It took everything she could do to keep from screaming.

Watching over the snowplow blade, Chet saw what was happening. He capped the bottle of green paint and rushed up into the cab with Natalie.

Meanwhile, squatting next to Wayne, Stubblefield sniffed the air like a hound, acting suspicious. He reached out with a french fry and dragged it through the ketchup covering Wayne. He sniffed the fry, then popped it into his mouth.

Up in the snowplow's cab, Natalie and Chet tried to quiet Trudy down. Then Trudy opened her beak and warbled her little head off, perfectly mimicking a high-pitched car alarm.

Stubblefield stood and turned around at once, spotting Natalie and Chet. They spotted him right back, and it was a glaring contest through the dirty windshield.

"Get out of my truck!" Snowplowman commanded.

With a last desperate grab, Natalie managed to snare Trudy out of the air. She hopped out of the snowplow and landed on the street as Stubblefield started for them. Holding Trudy in both hands, her fingers encircling the little bird's tiny neck meaningfully, Natalie held the parakeet up like a cross to a vampire.

"Trudy!" Stubblefield screamed, slowing down his approach. "No! Let her go!"

"You want her," Natalie screamed back at him, "come and get her, dirtbag!" She turned and fled, followed by Chet, who hesitated only long enough to say, "Thank you and good night, everybody."

Stubblefield tried to follow, but even holding Trudy, who kept squawking, Natalie and Chet were too fast for him. However, as it turned out, Stubblefield *was* too fast for Wayne. The Snowplowman bounded back and grabbed Wayne before he had time to make his escape. He jerked Wayne up and hustled him toward the snowplow cab.

Hal stood at the railing at Crowley Rink.

Even though they were supposed to be broken up, Claire and Chuck were like the king and queen of winter out on the ice. Surprisingly, even with it being a snow day, the kids skated in an orderly counterclockwise circle. Primarily, though, that was because Mr. Zellweger, the ancient rink manager, only played really old music.

Then, when Chuck tried to put his arm around Claire and she shoved it away, Hal saw a little ray of hope. Lane joined him then. He didn't know if she'd seen Claire push Chuck's arm away or not, and he didn't ask. Lane seemed to be having her own problems with what was developing, and he didn't want her to get upset. He needed her for his plan.

She looked anxious and guilty.

"Did you do it?" he asked.

"Yeah." She glumly handed Hal a black Magic Marker. "My parents had such high hopes for me."

"You ready for part two?"

She made a face.

"Come on," he wheedled. "If you won't do it for me, do it for them." He pointed to the skaters. "How many years has Mr. Zellweger been putting everybody to sleep with that old fogey music?"

She glanced at the office overlooking the rink. Maybe she felt a little sorry for the manager. He was a little old guy in a neck brace. He seemed totally entranced by the music, tapping his fingers in time with it.

"Of course," Mr. Zellweger said over the microphone in that flat, totally unexcited monotone of his, "that was 'Love Letters' by the Sultan of Smooth, Mr. Al Martino. While we're still in a romantic mood, skaters are reminded that there's no better way to say 'I love you' than with a brand-new pair of skate guards. On sale in the main office." He put another record on the player, and an equally boring song came on. "Hey, are you ready to party? I know I am. So let's make the scene, Gene, as—who else?—Al Martino invites us into a world of 'Fascination.' "

One of the kids actually fell asleep on his skates, crashed into the railing, and flipped over the bar. That definitely indicated some action should be taken. Hal glanced at Lane.

Lane rolled her eyes and stamped her foot, then walked toward the rink office.

Hal turned his attention back to Claire and Chuck. They were so close that he could hear them talking.

"I can't skate to this," Claire told Chuck. She pulled into the railing not far from where Hal stood.

"Let me take care of it," Chuck said, stopping beside her. He turned around, cupped his hands, and shouted at Mr. Zellweger. "Hey, old man, how about playing some Metallica? Metallica! Metallica!" He glanced back at Claire, really trying to put out the charm now. "Whatever it takes, babe, 'cause, when you're happy, I'm happy. When you're sad"— Chuck went to sad, but it was way over the top—"I know you don't think of me as Mr. Sensitive, but it eats me up inside."

Hal didn't think Claire was buying his little production anyway, but Chuck really blew it when Bill Korn happened to skate by. "Hey, zip. This is for earlier." Chuck stepped forward and body-slammed

Bill into the boards, knocking him completely off his feet.

Claire groaned disgustedly. "Chuck," she said in a sharp voice, "can I ask you a question?"

"Ask away." Chuck didn't even notice she was upset with him.

"Who am I?"

Chuck smiled. "You're my woman."

"No," Claire replied. "Who am I as a person? We've been dating three years. What do you really know about me?"

A worried look settled into Chuck's usually worry-free face, and Hal grinned. *Snow day magic, that's what it has to be. The stars are lining up.*

"Wow," Chuck said. "Heavy. Okay, well . . . I know your favorite animal is the chimpanzee. You're absolutely crazy about chimps."

Claire scowled at him.

"Spider monkeys?" Chuck asked with less confidence.

Hal knew the answer. He still had her bracelet in his pocket. But he had to wait till the time was right. Lane was working on the timing even now, and he needed to be ready to move.

At the rink office, Lane banged on the door with a fist and used her best frantic voice. It was a stretch, because frantic was something Lane Leonard usually didn't do. "Mr. Zellweger? Mr. Zellweger, please! It's an emergency."

Even then Mr. Zellweger was slow about poking his head out the door. Over the years a lot of kids had tried to prank on him in retaliation for the boring music he insisted on playing. "What seems to be the problem?"

Lane acted totally freaked. "In the ladies room—" She grabbed her chest and made big eyes. "Oh, my God, I tried to stop her—Lord knows I tried."

"Stop who?" Mr. Zellweger asked, kind of getting into the frantic thing himself. "From doing what?"

"Al Martino bites the big one," Lane told him. "That's what she wrote. In the bathroom stall. Some weird girl with a dog collar and a snake tattooed on her face. And she's still there, Mr. Zellweger. Who knows what she's writing now?"

Mr. Zellweger took the bait and a vein began throbbing on his forehead. "What kind of sicko—" He struggled to regain control of himself. "Take me to her. Now!"

Lane took the lead and they dashed off.

Hal headed straight for the office and let himself in.

Chapter 12

On the way to the rink, Hal had discovered a CD in the pocket of his coat. He'd borrowed it from Lane a few days back and forgotten to return it. Snow day magic, it had to be. He pulled it out of his pocket.

Chuck was hip deep in quicksand and sinking quickly as he tried to make up with Claire. "I remember now," he was saying. "What are those things that have the bright red butts? Baboons!"

Claire closed her eyes. "Chuck, what color are my eyes?"

Chuck didn't even hesitate. "They're green, of course."

Claire opened her eyes and shook her head in disbelief.

Chuck got a good look at those eyes then. "That darker shade of green that looks a lot like brown," he said, trying to cover. "I'm completely on top of it."

"One last question," Claire said. "What flavor gum do I chew?"

Chuck didn't even try to answer, and Claire skated off almost immediately. He stood there, getting madder. Marla, one of Claire's buddies, skated by and he turned on her. "'What flavor gum do I chew?' What kind of bogus question is that?" he demanded.

Marla shrugged and smiled a little. "The kid on TV knew the answer."

"What kid on TV?"

Marla pointed at Hal, who was standing behind the big glass window in the rink office. "Him," she said.

Hal grinned and yanked the needle off the Perry Como record. He took the microphone, feeling more comfortable with this one than the one earlier, and said, "May I have your attention, please."

Every head in the rink turned to look at him. It was a great feeling, because one of those heads belonged to Claire.

"Thank you," he went on. "Due to circumstances beyond his control, Mr. Zellweger can't be with us right now."

Mr. Zellweger was in the girls' bathroom with Lane. The *culprit* had made a clean getaway, of course, but Mr. Zellweger was cleaning the Magic Marker graffiti off the stall with a pencil eraser. A very small pencil eraser, Lane noticed.

82

"What is wrong with today's youth?" Mr. Zellweger demanded.

Lane didn't have an answer.

Hal locked eyes with Claire, keeping up his chatter. "So to continue the party mood, I'd like to make a special snow day dedication to . . . Claire Bonner. Hi. You might think I'm crazy, Claire, but that's okay." He hit Play, starting up "You Might Think," by the Cars.

The song was loud and fast, irresistible to everyone who'd been going to Crowley Rink for years. Every skater started moving, yelling and screaming in sheer enjoyment. A mosh pit formed immediately.

Well, maybe not every skater joined in. Claire and the other cools in her group eased out of the pack of wild skaters. It looked as if Claire wasn't really ready to leave and her friends dragged her away, but Hal couldn't be sure of that. He hoped so. *Surely we share a taste in music.*

She looked at Hal, kind of surprised, like she was seeing him for the very first time. Then Chuck smashed against the booth glass, slamming his palms and making it impossible to see anything but him. "You . . . are . . . so . . . dead!" he screamed over the loud music.

"Sorry, Chuck," Hal said, grinning a grin that just wouldn't go away. "Can't hear you." He had some volume left on the knobs, so he cranked it up some more.

Chuck roared and slapped the glass even harder.

Someone poked Hal in the side. For a second there his heart almost stopped, thinking Mr. Zellweger was back already.

But it was only Lane. She looked at Hal, a little worried. "Hal, we gotta get outta here. I think the Chuck Wheeler House of Pain is officially open for business."

Hal thought so too, and he'd accomplished what he set out to do. He took Lane's hand and they ran out of the rink office and through the back door.

Wayne was terrified, holding his hands over his head as he sat beside Stubblefield in the snowplow cab. Stubblefield raised the big blade so he could make better time, constantly looking out over the houses to try to find Trudy and the birdnappers.

"Snowplowman," Wayne said. "I mean *Mr.* Snowplowman, I was just wondering. That story about how you frequently grind kids into road salt . . ." He hesitated, then laughed as if he got the joke. "That's just a story, right?"

Stubblefield gave him a hard look.

Wayne nodded, more afraid than ever. "You can get back to me on that one. No rush." He reached for the door handle, then whimpered when he realized there wasn't one. He whispered, "I'm toast."

While Wayne was entertaining Snowplowman, Natalie and Chet were streaking through the neighborhood, trying to stay out of his sight. The last street they had to cross was a bit of a miscalculation. It took longer to sprint across than they thought, and Darling Clementine was just making the corner when they had ten feet to go.

She and Chet threw themselves forward and tumbled into the yard. They skidded across the snow and smacked up against the side of a house, then flattened and watched Stubblefield cruise by slowly.

"Phew," Natalie gasped, trying to get her wind back. "That was close."

Inside Chet's coat, Trudy went crazy for a moment, scratching and clawing.

"Take it easy in there," Chet ordered.

"He's going right to my house," Natalie said, peering down the street. "I knew it."

"You're sure Snowplowman's not going to rat on us?" Chet asked.

"No way," Natalie answered. "He knows better. He tells and he won't get his stupid bird back." She started to walk away.

Chet didn't follow, holding his pants. "Uh, Natalie?"

"Yeah?"

"The bird is in my pants." Suddenly, Chet's pants exploded with movement. "Owwwww!"

Natalie shook her head. "Quit messing around, willya? If we're going to get Wayno back, we gotta move quick." She trudged off again.

Laura punched the same key on the board again and again while talking to Nona. "I don't know why it's not printing, Nona. Come on. I need these cost projections."

"Mom? Mom?" Randy called from the playroom.

"I'll be right there, honey!" Laura called back. "I know I have paper in the printer, so what's the problem?" She slid the paper tray open to make sure. She gazed down at the peanut butter and bologna sandwich lying inside. Only one tiny bite had been taken out of it. She couldn't believe it.

"Mom? Mom?" Randy called.

"I said I'll be right there, Randy!"

"Mrs. Huffner said it's not nice to lie!"

Laura felt completely overwhelmed. "Nona, I have to call you back." She broke the phone connection and hurried to the playroom. "All right, now. Let mommy see what her little artist has been up to."

When she saw the room, she thought she was going to have a nervous breakdown. Blue paint covered the walls, the sofa, the TV, the BarcaLounger, the rug, the bookshelf, the lamp, and the fishbowl. Randy stood in the middle of it all, buck naked and just as blue.

"Can I go outside now?" he asked.

Before Laura could catch her breath, the doorbell rang.

When she answered the door, one of the roughest men Laura had ever seen in her life stood there. If she hadn't seen Wayne sitting in Darling Clementine, she wouldn't have opened the door.

"Ma'am," Stubblefield said politely. "Sorry to intrude on your afternoon. I wonder if you might be able to tell me where I could find your daughter."

"Natalie?" Laura was confused. This man wasn't the kind to come to a door unless there was trouble. "Why? Is she in some kind of trouble?"

"No, no, no. Nothing like that. A bunch of kids in the neighborhood signed up for free rides in the plow and your Natalie is next on the list."

Laura glanced at the huge snowplow out in the street. "Oh, hey, you're the guy the kids call Snow-plowman, aren't you?"

Stubblefield smiled. "Kids have a lot of different names for me. You can call me Roger."

Laura peered over his shoulder at Wayne, seated in Darling Clementine. "Okay, Roger. Is that Wayne Alworth?"

"Why, yes, it is." Snowplowman was a quick thinker. "We just finished his ride."

Out in Darling Clementine, Wayne beeped the horn frantically.

Stubblefield shook his head and laughed. "How they love to toot the horn."

Wayne scribbled furiously on the window, marking letters in the condensation.

"What's he writing?" Laura asked. "PLEH?"

Chapter 13

Stubblefield looked at Wayne in Darling Clementine's cab with his ꟼ⅃ƎH sign marked in condensation, then glanced back at Laura. "It's a plowing term I taught him. Kind of technical." He stepped forward, blocking Laura's view. "Ma'am, if you don't mind, a lot of kids are still on the list, so if you could just tell me where your daughter is—"

Randy broke through their defensive line like it was nothing, interrupting them. In a heartbeat he was outside in the front yard jumping up and down, still buck naked.

"Randy!" Laura shrilled. "Get back here! Awww!" She stepped through the door after Randy.

Stubblefield pointed a warning finger at Wayne, who wiped the message from the glass. The phone rang, loud in the suddenly quiet house. The ringing continued, so he walked over to the phone. "Hello?"

Natalie and Chet were across the street at Chet's house. Natalie had made the call as soon as she saw Randy streak for the front yard. She hadn't known how she was going to get by her mom without having her voice recognized, but the snow day magic kicked in. She just took advantage of it.

"Hello, Snowplowman," Natalie said over the phone. "There's someone here who wants to say hi to you." She held the phone close to Chet's coat and Trudy whistled.

"Trudy?" Stubblefield said. "Are you okay? They haven't hurt you, have they?"

"Not yet," Natalie said.

"What do you want from me?"

"Oh, I don't know. What do you think, Chet?" He shrugged. Natalie made her voice harder to Stubblefield. "How about we get our friend back and you give us a second snow day?"

"Never," Stubblefield replied at once.

"Then we keep the bird and you keep the Wayne," Natalie told him easily. She watched him through the window.

Stubblefield turned and looked toward Darling Clementine where Wayne was gouging at an ear with his finger. Wayne mined a ball of wax from his ear, then spent a long time trying to flick it off.

Stubblefield sounded beaten. "All right. What do you want me to do?"

Natalie was smiling. Dr. Freon had never given up this easily. "Muller's field. Twenty minutes. And no funny stuff."

A few minutes later, Natalie and Chet were in the middle of Muller's field, waiting for Stubblefield to arrive. She was positively gloating and couldn't wait to stare Snowplowman down. He wasn't even in the same league as Dr. Freon.

Chet was laughing, pacing energetically. "And to think we used to be afraid of this joker."

Natalie grinned. "How easy is this? We give him the bird, he gives us an extra snow day?"

"Why stop there?" Chet asked. "I say we go for two. No, three."

"Yeah!" Natalie enthused. "Three snow days and I get to drive his truck."

"Three snow days," Chet said, upping the ante, "you get to drive his truck, and he has to keep the Wayne."

Both of them laughed, totally enjoying the idea of the coming battle. She took Meltar out of her pocket. "If Hal could see us now, eh, Meltar? We'd show him how to save the universe."

Chet kept pacing. "Where is this mook? He should be here by now."

Natalie held Meltar up to the wind. "He'll be here." She changed her voice to Meltar's. "Just listen to the wind."

But the wind wasn't what they heard in the next second. What they heard was Wayne screaming over the dulled *ker-chunk* of Darling Clementine's spiked tires.

"That's not the wind," Chet whispered, peering through the trees at the end of the street.

Then Darling Clementine came into view, black smoke roiling from the stack. The snowplow turned toward Natalie and Chet. Wayne was still screaming, and he was strapped to the front of the plow.

Natalie couldn't believe it.

Stubblefield braked the snowplow only a few feet away. "Sorry if I'm late," he yelled out the open window of the cab, "but I had to pick up a friend."

Natalie couldn't say anything.

Stubblefield opened the door and stepped down from the cab, landing in the snowy street. He walked toward Natalie. "Let's get this over with. Gimme the bird."

"Gimme the Wayne," Natalie responded.

"Bird."

"Wayne."

"You first."

"*You* first."

"I said 'you first' first."

"So." Natalie didn't give him anything.

Wayne struggled against the straps holding him to Darling Clementine's plow. "Just give him the bird. Please? I want to go home."

"Do it," Chet said, scared, "so we can get out of here."

Reluctantly, Natalie opened the oatmeal carton

and released the parakeet. Trudy flew to Stubblefield immediately.

"Hey, girl," Stubblefield said. "Welcome home. Did you miss me?"

The parakeet chirped happily.

Wayne struggled against the bindings that held him and almost succeeded in getting away.

"Not so fast, porky." Snowplowman yanked the straps and dropped Wayne into the snow. He grabbed Wayne and shoved him forward. Then just as quickly snatched him back.

"Nooooo!" Wayne yelled in helpless fright.

"Let him go!" Natalie exploded.

Stubblefield grinned. "But we've been having so much fun together, haven't we, Wayne?"

Wayne whimpered. "Yeah. Sort of."

Stubblefield pointed to the snowplow's door with pride. Twenty snowflakes were painted on it, each one stylized. "In fact I was just telling him a cute little story about these snowflakes here. Pretty, huh? I painted them myself. Each one marks a snow day that I personally plowed into oblivion. This one here." He touched one of the snowflakes affectionately. "Thirty-six inches. A real hoo-ha." He pointed to another snowflake. "This one's from three years ago. January seventh, I believe."

"Every school in the county was closed except for ours," Natalie stated dully.

Stubblefield nodded. "What can I say? I'm good."

"It's true, isn't it? You never had a snow day."

Snowplowman's expression softened just a little.

"No. I used to think if I got enough of these," he said, gesturing toward the painted snowflakes, "maybe someday I could get on with my life. But then one day I realized this *is* my life." He shoved Wayne into the snow in front of them. "So stay out of it."

"Hey, Dan," Tom called out as he headed toward the counter at Dan's Diner. Now dressed as Jack Frost, he drew a lot of attention. He dropped onto a stool at the counter. "I'll have a coffee. Black."

Dan tried not to laugh. "Well, looky here. Who are you supposed to be now?"

"I'm Abraham Lincoln, Dan," Tom replied. "America's most beloved president. Vote for me."

"You're some kind of snow elf, aren't you?" Dan growled. "I know, old Jack Frost, am I right?" He cracked up.

"Just give me the coffee."

Dan continued laughing as he poured the coffee.

Tom shook his head and noticed a kid at the counter staring at him. "Ever seen a grown elf cry?"

The kid looked at him blankly, then went back to staring at the television above the counter.

Tom heard the familiar theme song from the Channel 10 news promo. He glanced up at the television in irritation. It further annoyed him to notice that everyone in the diner was watching. The scene was of a howling rainstorm.

"Who was there when El Niño went el loco?" the television announcer asked.

"Chad Symmonz!" everyone in the diner yelled out.

Tom groaned, feeling lower than low.

Footage of a tornado rolled across the screen. "Who was there when a killer tornado devastated downtown?"

"Chad Symmonz!" the diner crowd yelled, louder than ever.

Tom got even angrier.

On the screen, footage rolled of the snowstorm that had hit Syracuse last night. "And who was there last night when the blizzard of the century came knocking on our door?"

"Chad Symmonz!" everyone in the diner answered.

Before Dan could stop him, Tom grabbed the remote control and smashed it against the counter. When the diner got quiet, he looked up, embarrassed. "On second thought, Dan, maybe I've had enough coffee." He handed the remote to the diner owner. "Here you go." He headed for the door, noticing a girl who looked familiar.

"Hey, Mr. Brandston," Lane called out to him. "Love the hat!"

Lane took the stool where Tom had sat. She looked anxiously at Claire's little gathering in the power booth. Normally, those people avoided her and she returned the favor. Bill Korn was sitting beside her, building a log house out of french fries. "Bill."

"Hey, check it out," Bill said enthusiastically. "A french fry log cabin."

"You're not wasting your day," Lane said sarcastically.

"You know it," Bill said. "So what's going on? Where's Hal?"

"The football field," Lane answered without enthusiasm. She'd left him there with a snow shovel, furiously digging in the snow so he could complete his big project before she returned with Claire. "He's off building some kind of shrine to the Lady Claire." Lane glanced at Claire. She took up her milk shake when Dan put it in front of her and sipped. "And I'm the feeb who's been sent here to fetch her."

Bill kept building. "Rock on."

Lane sipped the milk shake again, then glanced over at the power booth.

Paula was talking. "Okay, so we've ruled out food poisoning, allergies, temporary insanity . . . "

"How about frostbite?" Fawn asked. "Maybe you're not wearing enough layers."

Claire looked at her friends. "How about that I just might actually think the guy is cute?"

Fawn started choking on her food.

Marla's response was immediate. "How about that you're on the verge of committing total social suicide?"

Claire rolled her eyes.

Before anyone could think of anything to say, Principal Weaver suddenly slammed against the window right next to them, gasping. He begged someone to help him. No one made a move. Then a hundred snowballs came out of nowhere and slammed into the principal, forcing him back out into the street and on his way again. Business in Dan's Diner returned to normal.

Marla was the first to get her voice back. "All right. Just for fun, let's pretend that for some unknown reason you *like* this guy. What do you know about him?"

Screwing up her courage and putting her pride on a back burner, Lane decided to make her move. She crossed the diner, ignoring the stares that trailed after her, and dropped into the booth across from Claire.

Chapter 14

"He's very ticklish," Lane told Claire and her friends. But she was speaking directly to Claire. "I can tell you that."

All of them just stared at her.

Lane didn't let them see how nervous she was. She reached out and snagged a cheese fry from Marla's plate, never letting on that she knew Marla, Paula, and Fawn were looking at her as if she had some kind of disease. Only Claire seemed to be listening with interest.

"What else?" Lane asked rhetorically, then kept on speaking. "He hates drum machines, he does a great Eeyore impression. Oh, yeah, he once gave mouth-to-mouth resuscitation to a baby chick. Seriously. It was Easter, and my mom got the bright idea of bringing baby chicks home for everyone. It was kind of cute until they all started croaking, which they always seem to do right after you name them. Anyway, there's Hal on his hands and knees giving mouth-to-mouth—or mouth-to-beak, in this case—to my bird. It was very *ER.*" She watched the three girls watching her, savoring the moment because she had them speechless.

Marla, Paula, and Fawn weren't amused, but Lane knew she was getting to Claire by the way Claire was smiling.

"He also likes rainbows and people who are nice," Lane finished.

"Don't you have something better to do?" Fawn demanded.

"Yeah," Paula added, "like fix that hathead."

Lane had been so concerned about how to present Hal, she hadn't even thought of herself. When she touched the hathead ridge in her hair, she wanted to groan, but she didn't, because she was that strong. "Didn't you hear?" she asked. "Flat hair is very *in* this year."

Marla spoke harshly. "You. Leaving. Now."

Lane ignored her and plunged ahead. "I'm going, but, Claire, you've got to come with me. Hal is expecting you."

Claire raised her eyebrows.

"Look," Lane went on, "I know you hardly even know the guy, but all I can tell you is that you know when you're making a snow angel and you want to make it perfect but you can't because you always leave a handprint when you climb out?"

Claire nodded, not sure where all this was headed.

"Well," Lane said, "with Hal, there's no hand-print." She hoped that was intriguing enough to get Claire moving.

Claire stood and pulled her coat on.

Paula looked as if she'd just found something crawling through the cheese fries. "Claire, you're making a big mistake."

"What about Chuck?" Marla asked. "What's he going to think?"

"Chuck doesn't think," Claire told them. And she left with Lane.

Chuck Wheeler sped through the Slupperton Hill neighborhood on his souped-up snowmobile. He had Steve and Greg, two of his friends, with him on their own snowmobiles.

They found the polar explorer first. Chuck skidded to a stop beside the kid, who was pulling his dog in the saucer sled. Chuck showed the polar explorer a picture of Hal Brandston he'd cut out of the school yearbook. "We're looking for this guy. Have you seen him around?"

The polar explorer took the picture and looked at it. "Commander Scott!" he said. "Confound him and the dogsled he came in on!" He turned to the beagle. "Onward, Roscoe! We dare not tarry with Scott afoot and the pole so near! Mush, I say!"

Chuck and his buddies watched the polar explorer tug the saucer sled away and didn't have a clue about what was going on. Chuck climbed back onto his snowmobile and took off again.

Only a little farther on, they found Bill Korn. Bill didn't even see them. He was busy making snowballs, throwing them up in the air, then standing underneath them so they smashed against his head. The sound of the approaching snowmobiles caught his attention.

Bill couldn't believe Chuck and his buddies would be interested in him. But no one else was around. Hoping to make them lose interest in him, he made a huge snowball, threw it into the air, then let it crash down on his head and shoulders. He wobbled, pretending to be stunned, then fell over into the snow and lay there.

The only problem was, Chuck and his friends didn't get bored and ride away. That let Bill know they were definitely after him. When they started approaching slowly, he scrambled to his feet and took off.

Bill didn't stand a chance against the snowmobiles, even dodging around the houses. Chuck drove by and kicked a leg out, knocking Bill's feet out from under him. Before Bill could get back up, Chuck had jumped off the snowmobile and put a knee in his chest, holding him down on the ground. A melting icicle clinging to the side of the house splattered drops on Bill's forehead.

Chuck showed Bill the picture.

"I don't know where he is!" Bill said, trying to turn his head away from the steady drip of the icicle. "I swear!"

"I believe you." Greg leaned forward, pinning Bill

under the icicle. The icicle started to creak and groan as it pulled loose from the house and got ready to drop onto Bill.

"He's at the stadium!" Bill screamed when he couldn't take it anymore. "The stadium! The stadium!"

Out on the football field, Hal heaved one last shovelful of snow on top of his creation and looked around. Despite the chill in the air, he was covered with sweat. His back, arms, legs, and shoulders ached as never before.

But the pain went away when he saw Lane and Claire enter the top of the bleachers. Even from a distance, he could see the surprise on Claire's face. It made every one of those pains and aches worthwhile.

"You should see what he can do when he's really trying," Lane said

In the time Lane had been gone, Hal had whipped together a 100-yard-long whale that looked remarkably like the charm on Claire's bracelet. Even if he had to say so himself, it looked pretty good. He'd even added radiant lines around it so it would glow.

"You made this for me?" Claire shouted to him.

Hal nodded.

"Why?"

Hal felt troubled. *Surely she understands.* "It's your favorite animal. A whale." He paused. "You know, nature's gentle giant."

101

"But I like zebras."

Hal couldn't believe it. No way could this be happening. He held up the ankle bracelet. "Then how come you have a whale charm on your bracelet?"

"You've got my bracelet?" Claire turned to Lane. "How did he get my bracelet?"

"Destiny," Lane answered sarcastically, "pure destiny."

Then the popping roar of snowmobile engines filled the stadium. Chuck and his two friends roared onto the field.

"Oh, no!" Claire exclaimed.

Chuck fishtailed to a stop in front of Hal, who'd only had a brief time to consider running before he was cut off.

"Hey, zip, you're in luck!" Chuck sang. "The House of Pain now delivers." He grabbed Hal by the collar.

"Chuck!" Claire yelled. "What do you want!"

"Claire bear!" Chuck said, whipping around and letting Hal go. "I've been looking all over for you!" He turned back to Hal. "As for you, Mr. Wonderful . . ." Then he noticed the bracelet Hal was holding. "Hey, what do you have there?" He grabbed the bracelet. "Ewww. It's all sweaty. This is Claire's. I gave it to her. What are you doing with it?"

"I can explain," Hal said, not sure if he could.

Chuck looked to Claire. "Claire, what's this dink doing with your bracelet?"

She shrugged.

Chuck looked at Hal. "I wouldn't want to be you

in about two minutes." He turned his attention back to Claire. "Don't worry, we'll get this back on your lovely ankle without delay." He gazed at her fondly. "Remember when I gave this to you? At Aqua Land. They had the glass-bottom boat, remember?"

Claire smiled and Hal felt his heart breaking.

"The tour guide kept telling us to gaze upon the exotic wonders of the deep," Chuck went on. "All I did was look at you."

Claire's grin grew even bigger.

Hal seized the moment, knowing Chuck's attention was totally on Claire. Moving slowly, he headed for one of the idling snowmobiles.

"Why did you buy me a whale?" Claire asked Chuck. "I've always wanted to know."

"Because of Shampoo," Chuck answered.

A puzzled look replaced Claire's smile.

"Shampoo the killer whale," Chuck said. "You loved that whale."

"It's not Shampoo, you blowhole," Hal stated. "It's Shamu."

Claire giggled and Chuck turned beet-red. But he also turned around too late to do anything other than see Hal sprinting for the snowmobile.

"Don't even think about it!" Chuck roared.

Hal ignored him, dropping onto the seat and grabbing the handlebars. He twisted the throttle and the snowmobile sped into motion.

Chuck sprinted for his own snowmobile, shouting to Claire over his shoulder. "It can be like it was, Claire."

"Chuck, we broke up."

"Yeah, but not technically. We'll talk about it." Chuck turned around and threw everything he had into catching Hal.

Hal didn't wait for Chuck, opening the throttle as much as he dared and speeding across the snow. Thankfully, he got the gearshift lever to drop into place so he could go even faster. The tracked belt surged at the back of the snowmobile and for a minute the vehicle reared almost straight up. He leaned forward instinctively, putting the front skis back on the ground. Then he was off, racing for his life while Chuck, Greg, and Steve followed on the other snowmobiles.

Chapter
15

The football blocking sled came out of nowhere in front of Hal while he was working desperately to keep the snowmobile right side up. One minute the blocking sled wasn't there, and the next it was. He had enough trouble just handling the unfamiliar snowmobile without running an obstacle course too. He barely got around the sled, but Chuck and Steve had no problem at all.

Now out of the stadium and driving through a practice field, they sped up beside Hal on either side and closed in.

"You are quite the ladies' man, aren't you?" Chuck called out. "Greg, say hello."

Greg, riding shotgun on Chuck's snowmobile, reached out and grabbed Hal's shoulder. "Hi, I'm Greg. I'll be hurting you this afternoon."

Hal felt Greg's grip tighten and knew he was

going to try to pull him off the snowmobile. When they topped a small hill, Hal saw that they were headed for a tree.

Barely recovering in time, Hal swerved and missed the tree. Chuck powered around it as well, but Greg wasn't so fortunate. A large branch smacked him from the snowmobile.

Hal also lost his balance, almost falling off the snowmobile. As Hal hung on for dear life, Chuck raised a booted foot and started kicking at Hal's hands. "Here, let me give you a hand."

Hal struggled to maintain control and keep his hands out of the way. Luckily, Chuck had to swerve again to avoid a blocking sled. Hal took the opportunity to pull himself back up onto the speeding machine.

But Chuck closed in again, grinning to bare his teeth.

Hal just about gave it up then and there, but then he noticed the soccer net out of the corner of his eye. The bravery of Fangor descended on him at that moment. He pulled the handlebars and veered hard left.

Chuck never even saw the net until he was in it. The snowmobile came to an abrupt stop that ripped Chuck right out of the seat.

Hal kept going, knowing Chuck and his buddies would recover quickly. But he had a chance to add to his lead. He sped up Slupperton Hill just past the stadium. *I'm going to make it; I'm really going to make it.*

Then Principal Weaver stepped out in front of

him. "Aaaahhhhh!" the man yelled, only a few steps ahead of the barrage of snowballs that followed him.

"Aaaahhhhh!" Hal yelled in response. He yanked the handlebars hard, barely missing the principal. Snowballs pursued the man.

Then the ground fell away beneath Hal.

In the next instant he was airborne. Sleds, toboggans, and saucers were scattered over the snow-covered ground. Miraculously, he didn't come down on any of them. But he wasn't exactly in control of the snowmobile either.

Tom stood in front of the Susan B. Anthony Middle School doing another telecast. He moved slowly through a display of snow and ice sculptures the Cub Scouts had made. The film crew stood in front of him, shooting the scene as the telecast went out live.

"Hello there, Syracuse," Tom greeted the at-home audience. "Well, winter is finally here, and you know what that means: ice sculptures, Cub Scouts, and a big idiot dressed up like a magic elf."

In the control room back at the television station, Tina Stillman shook her head as she watched the live broadcast. "He's losing it. Come on, Tom, pull it together. You can do it."

Tom walked over to the sculptures and the camera followed him. A Cub Scout was standing beside each sculpture. "That's right. Old Jack Frost here, taking you on a tour of this year's Winter Jamboree." He pointed out a sculpture shaped like a moose. "Wow. Will you look at that? Nice moose there, young fellow. Wouldn't mind having that in my den." He laughed. "It's amazing what some kids will do for a merit badge, isn't it?" Tom allowed the cameraman to follow him, showing the sculptures of a large, ornate swan, a big fish, an igloo, and a Volkswagen. Then he saw a sculpture he just couldn't believe. "Oh, give me a break!"

The fifteen-foot-tall ice sculpture bore an amazing resemblance to Chad Symmonz, even though the scout couldn't have had much time to create it.

While Tom was standing there stunned, the eager scout beside the sculpture came up, still holding a hammer and chisel. "It's Chad Symmonz," the scout said proudly. "Whenever there's weather that affects our area, he's there first."

Regaining some of his composure, Tom said, "Kids, as unpredictable as the weather." He reached for the hammer. "Mind if I borrow that?" He grabbed the hammer, preparing to definitely alter the statue's features.

"Hey," the scout protested. He jumped up and down, trying to get the hammer back.

Tom held the hammer away. "It's for your own good. Now just get out of my way."

"Stop, you nut job!"

Tom lifted the hammer, prepared to pulverize

the sculpture. The sound of a revved-up engine screaming just short of exploding drew his attention. When he looked up and saw Hal blasting through the nearby trees and approaching like a runaway train, he couldn't believe it. "Judas Priest on a pony."

Chapter 16

Still being chased by Chuck Wheeler, Hal ripped through the intersection in front of the Susan B. Anthony Middle School, going way too fast. For a few seconds there, Tom just knew his son was going to pile up against the side of the Channel 6 Action Weather van. *Film at eleven.*

The earphone crackled in his ear, and Tina was shouting. "No! Don't even tell me he's back!"

But Hal *was* back, and he was still going. Tom watched as Hal, by some miracle, managed to veer away, weaving in between the sculptures and sending people fleeing for their lives.

Having slowed down, Hal was able to gain some control and shut off the snowmobile. He coasted over in front of the Chad Symmonz sculpture, barely tapping the base.

"Hal," Tom said.

"Dad," Hal replied, looking kind of surprised that he was still alive.

"Chad!" the young scout screamed.

Tom gave a sigh of relief—till he saw the huge Chad Symmonz sculpture slowly topple over. Hal barely had time to get out of the way before the sculpture totally crushed the snowmobile. Broken chunks of icy Chad Symmonz rained down all over.

Unable to keep the smile completely from his face, Tom turned to face the camera. "Well, Phyllis, that about wraps it up from here. Back to you."

Back at home, Natalie sat dejectedly on the bed in Hal's room. The afternoon light struck the panels on the collection of action figures. The only figure missing was Meltar, and Natalie was holding him, talking to him because Hal wasn't there.

"Sorry, Meltar. I thought I could do it without Hal. It doesn't matter. The universe is probably better off without us." She reached up and put him on the shelf, but she was halfway to the door when she heard a voice.

"Where in the name of the Seventh Sun are you going?" Meltar boomed.

Surprised, afraid she was completely losing it after what had happened with Stubblefield, Natalie turned around and watched Meltar stride out of the action figure case.

She knew she believed in the magic of snow day, but suddenly she started considering that she was believing way too much. She got over her surprise pretty quickly. After all, she knew of one way and one way only to deal with anyone who tried to tell her what to do. "To the kitchen," she snapped. "I'm gonna go make a grilled cheese sandwich."

Meltar gave her an angry look.

"What do you want me to say, Meltar?" Natalie demanded. "I lost. Evil won. The end."

At that moment, Tendrilla and Arcticon stepped out of the shadows of the action figure display case. "I lost. Evil won. Boo-hoo-hoo," Tendrilla taunted.

Arcticon snarled. "You think Meltar went home and ate a grilled cheese sandwich that day on Andromeda when he got ambushed by the Neutron Twins?"

Natalie started to feel bad. "No," she said a little more quietly.

"You're darn tootin' he didn't," Arcticon said.

Meltar interrupted quietly and politely. "If you two don't mind . . ."

Tendrilla and Arcticon turned to him apologetically. "Sorry. It's all yours. Take it away."

Meltar fixed his wise gaze on Natalie. "Natalie, there on Andromeda, things were looking pretty bleak. Like you, I too had lost my partner. Fangor had abandoned me to chase some space babe across the Forbidden Zone, and there I was, up Poop River without a paddle against those nasty Neutron Twins."

Natalie was surprisingly uninspired. First, because Meltar's troubles sounded so much like her own. And second, because this was a Meltar adventure she hadn't heard or taken part in before, so she didn't quite buy it. "Uh-huh," she said, sitting on the bed.

"Stranded there," Meltar said, "alone on the brink of extinction, I remembered a little saying I learned the first day at the Academy."

"Yeah, yeah, I know," Natalie groaned sarcastically. This part she had heard. " 'Winners never quit and quitters never win.' "

"No!" Meltar rumbled in his gravest tones. "It was 'Winners never quit, and quitters shall be cast into the flaming pit of death.' "

"Not fun," Tendrilla volunteered.

Arcticon agreed. "That's gotta sting."

"Look deep inside yourself, Natalie," Meltar advised. "Feel the rage of a hundred snow days that could have been, that would have been, if not for . . ."

"Snowplowman." Natalie blinked, and when she opened her eyes again, Meltar, Tendrilla, and Arcticon were all back in the shelves. But she still felt the burning deep in her gut. Not believing it had happened, unwilling to believe it was over, she plucked Meltar from the display case. Maybe the conversation had taken place in her imagination, but it had planted seeds of revenge within her that she couldn't ignore.

In her pseudo-office in the dining room, Laura paced back and forth in front of the window. The conference call was going to be the most important of her career and she knew it. From the safety of the computer monitor, Nona watched her worry.

"I got it," Nona said in triumph.

"Yesssss," Laura said. "What took you so long?"

"I had to go all the way down to Accounting, and there are no lights on and no people. It's spooky."

"As long as you found the file." Laura took a deep breath. "Nona, I can't believe I'm saying this, but I think we're ready to conquer China."

"Great. *Then* can I go home?"

Laura smiled. "Then you can go home."

Nona returned the smile, kicking out a foot and rolling her chair out of range of the video camera.

"Just make sure to patch me in when everyone in Beijing is ready," Laura said.

Nona rolled quickly back into camera view. "You're on in two minutes!" She looked panicked, then punched off the computer screen.

Laura looked at the materials spread across the desktop. "All right, here we go." She opened a folder. "Cost report, open." She pulled on her jacket. "Power suit, on." She glanced outside. "Randy, outside." She turned away from the window, her brain a couple steps behind her eyes. Suddenly she realized what she'd seen. She spun around and stared through the window again. "Randy! You come in here right now!"

Randy only waved at her, then took off down the driveway.

Totally panicked, Laura grabbed her cell phone and took off in pursuit.

Chapter 17

By the time Laura got outside, Randy had vanished. She stood in the driveway, searching for him. "Randy? Come back, honey! I'll let you paint anything you want blue! Even me! I promise!"

Just when she was about to give up, she spotted Randy's red snowsuit darting across the street. She went after him at once, but punched buttons on her cell phone at the same time, wondering how much of her two-minute warning was left.

"Nona?" she said into the cell phone. "Nona, it's me! Forget the video patch! Call me on the cell phone! Just do it! One minute. Right. One minute." Before she could put the cell phone away, a snowball whizzed out of nowhere and smashed into the phone, knocking it from her hand. "Noooooo!"

Laura had no idea where the cell phone had landed, but she bent down and started shifting snow at once. While she was bent over, Randy apparently couldn't resist such an easy target. Another snowball hit her in the rump.

Randy howled in glee, totally in his element in the snow. "Snowball fight!" he shrilled. "Come on, Mom! Fight back!"

"Stop it, Randy!" Laura yelled back. "It's very, very important that mommy finds her phone!"

She got no sympathy from Randy. He whipped up another snowball and plastered her again.

"Randall Todd Brandston! Enough is enough! Do you hear me?"

Randy smacked her with another snowball. He was really in the groove that day.

Laura hit him with her ultimate threat: "Do you want me to tell Mrs. Huffner about this? Do you? Then you've got three seconds to—" She totally lost it when the next snowball hit her in the forehead. Too much pressure, too much guilt—it all came together with a vengeance. She leaned down and packed a snowball herself. "That's it! You want to fight? I'll give you a fight!" She threw the snowball.

The snowball *thunked* into Randy's chest. Laura started to laugh, but Randy threw another snowball and hit her again. In the next instant, snowballs started filling the air and Laura's anger and frustration went totally away. She and Randy laughed and played, totally lost in snow day magic.

The cell phone rang, buried somewhere in the

depths of a snowdrift. Laura heard it, but she couldn't pinpoint where it was coming from. She lost herself for just an instant, becoming a corporate woman again. Then Randy hit her with another zinger. Instantly, she let go all of the pressure and raked up another snowball herself.

Randy turned and ran, but Laura's arm was just too good. They continued playing, fueled by snow day magic.

Later that afternoon, after he'd finished getting chewed out for the things Hal had done on the last remote, Tom stood in another part of the neighborhood waiting to do his take on the weather story. For the moment, however, Chad Symmonz, wearing a silk scarf and a camel hair jacket, commanded the attention of the crowd.

Tom was dressed as Old Man Winter. He got angrier and angrier as he watched Symmonz. "If I went over there right now and, say, hog-tied him with that scarf and then took his microphone and poked his soft parts until he started crying for his mama, would I get in trouble?"

A crewman glanced at him nervously.

"I mean," Tom went on, "hypothetically."

"Why don't we just go to another location?" the crewman asked. "He got here first."

Tom shook his head. "We're not going anywhere."

The Channel 10 weather superstar took his cue from his producer and started speaking. "I'm here on

West Burlington Street, or should I say Burrrrrling-ton Street, ha-ha, where it's good to see that this record snowfall hasn't stopped some of my weather fans from turning out." He walked to one of the scouts—the same one who'd done the Chad Sym-monz ice sculpture. "How do you like all this snow, sporto?"

"It's great," the scout replied.

"Caught you by surprise, didn't it?" Chad asked. "Don't worry, it caught a lot of people by surprise. Luckily I was in the right place at the right time." He chuckled. "Again."

Tom couldn't help it. He couldn't stay silent any longer. He walked toward Chad with a tight smile plastered to his face. "I'd expect nothing else from the area's number one meteorologist."

Chad glanced at him warily. "Why, thank you. Channel Six's Tom Brandston, everybody."

Back at the station, Tina Stillman shook her head. Today was definitely not turning out the way she'd hoped. She slumped back in her chair and opened a channel to the crew on-site where Tom was about to confront Chad Symmonz. She would either have to broadcast what was going on or lose all the remotes she'd scheduled.

"Roll the ugliness," she said in defeat.

Tom waved to the camera, stepping deeper into the frame. "Hi, folks." He turned back to Chad. "Hoo-eee, Chad, I've got to tell you, that storm last night sure had me fooled. How did you ever call that one? I mean, I've just got to know."

"Let's call it a hunch." Chad turned toward the camera.

"Oh, yeah," Tom said knowingly, "a hunch. That's just one of those things they can't teach you in meteorology school."

"You got that right."

"By the way, where did you go to school anyway? Let me guess . . . Big Dope U.?"

An angry look passed across Chad's face. The crowd shifted nervously. No one had ever confronted Chad Symmonz before.

Tom held his hands up. "Just kidding there, Chad. Wherever you went, I'm sure that's how you learned that an upper atmospheric shift like the one we saw last night can lead to a sudden two-point drop in the Fleeber Index."

"Of course," Chad answered, glancing at his producer who was making frenzied motions to get Tom off the air.

Tom shook his head. "There is no Fleeber Index, Chad."

The crowd's murmur grew even louder.

"Ha-ha," Chad tried. "Had you going there, didn't I? Of course it's the Fleener Index."

Tom buzzed a game-show negative, truly enjoying having the upper hand. Chad just seemed to wither in front of him. "I'm sorry, Chad. So close. The correct answer is: I made it all up."

Chad's face grew dark with anger. "Folks, I apologize for this. It seems that Old Man Winter here is going a bit senile." He drew circles around his ear with his finger.

"You're a fraud," Tom said.

"You're a joke," Chad replied.

"Uh-oh, folks," Tom said. "Looks like we've reached a stalemate. How can we break it? We could wrestle, or . . . I know." He scooped up a handful of snow. "If you're not a fraud, then I guess you'd be able to tell me where this comes from."

"Snow?" Chad snorted.

Tom nodded.

"Snow," Chad said. "The Eskimos have eleven words for snow. We have but one: snow." He paused, evidently reaching. "Where does it come from? Way up there." He pointed at the sky. "Where cold air in the upper atmosphere sweeps down from Canada." He swept out a hand. "Like a roller coaster heading down a hill." He put on a deeper voice. "Whoa, get out of my way, I'm from Canada, eh!" He laughed. "And after a process that Tom Brandston knows very well is classified, we get what we weathermen call *the white stuff.*"

Dead silence hung in the air when he stopped speaking.

"Like that?" Tom snapped his fingers.

Chad nodded. "Just like that." He snapped his fingers.

The crowd only stared at him, totally not with the whole scene.

"You're a loser," the Cub Scout said in the silence that followed. The crowd jeered Chad with him.

Chad turned to Tom. "Go away."

"I will," Tom said, "as soon as you tell me who really was there first last night when the blizzard of the century came knocking on our door, as you put it."

Chad, having no way out, spoke softly. "Tom Brandston."

"Who?" Tom asked.

Dan looked up at the television in the diner and smiled.

"Tom Brandston," Dan said.

"Come again?" Tom asked on the set.

In the television studio control room, Tina Stillman smiled as she watched the live broadcast. "Tom Brandston," she said.

"Sorry," Tom said, "I can't hear you."

Hal sneaked through one of the backyards near Claire's house. He wasn't sure where Chuck was, but he figured Chuck might be in the area. After all, where else would Claire go?

Then someone caught him in a tackle, knocking him to the ground, stirring up flurries of snow. He panicked at first, afraid it was Chuck or Greg or Steve. He was relieved to discover it was Lane. She sat on top of him, looking down at him.

"You really do have the reflexes of a dead cow," she said, laughing.

Instead of fighting back or hitting her with a sarcastic comment of his own, Hal just lay there, totally unhappy. "You have to stop doing that."

"So, um, tough break back at the stadium with Claire. Ouch! That had to sting."

"Nothing I can't handle."

Lane laughed some more. "Oh, come on, Hal. Let me bring you back." She imitated Claire's voice. " 'I like zebras.' "

Hal grimaced. "A minor setback."

Lane shook her head in disbelief. "What is your problem?"

"I still say I found that bracelet for a reason."

Lane got to her feet, angrier than Hal had ever seen her. "Spare me, Hal. Okay? I really don't want to hear another word about that crappy bracelet."

Hal got angry too, knowing he was on dangerous ground. They'd never been this mad at each other before. "It's not crappy."

"I'm warning you."

"What is it with you?" Hal demanded. "Do you think I don't know that all of this is completely insane? I know it is. You don't have to keep reminding me. But I have to do it . . . and I need your help."

She shook her head. "No way."

"Why not?"

"Forget it. It doesn't matter."

"Yes, it does."

Lane backed away from him, for the first time ever when a joke wasn't involved. "Just leave me alone. I can't believe I wasted a whole snow day on this."

Hal got angrier himself, wishing Lane could just understand what this meant to him. "Oh, what mind-blowing thing didn't happen today because I needed your help?"

"You don't want to know."

"Yes, Lane, I do! Tell me!" Hal was mad and worried all at the same time, thinking that maybe nothing would ever be the same again.

Lane reached out and grabbed him suddenly. For an instant he was afraid she might hit him. She looked into his eyes. "This," she said, and kissed him right on the lips.

Hal stopped breathing, totally shocked.

Lane quickly stepped away from him, looking just as surprised. "You're the one who said anything could happen. Surprise!" After an uncomfortable silence, she turned and walked away.

Hal didn't know what to do, what to think, or anything close to what to say. He stayed silent and still, watching her walk away.

Chapter
18

The walk to the gym, the cold air, knowing all the trouble he was probably in for interrupting his dad's job—none of it worked to clear Hal's mind. By the time he reached the gym where he figured Claire might have gone to go swimming, he was still in a fog.

Where did that kiss come from?

The gym was empty, but he followed the hallway back to the pool area, listening to the squish of his snowboots filling the corridor. He stopped at the glass door leading to the gym.

He spotted Claire at once, dressed in a swimsuit and walking toward the end of the high board. *Score one for the master sleuth! But you sure missed one of the big ones, didn't you?* It took the zing out of finding Claire there.

Seeing Claire in a swimsuit took his mind off

Lane, though. He watched as Claire bounced on the board, then did a double flip with a twist and entered the water with hardly a splash at all.

While Claire pulled herself out of the pool, he let himself through the door. She had already reached the board and was preparing for another dive when she spotted him.

"Every dive tells a story, you know," he said.

She looked down, a small smile on her lips. "I don't buy that for a second."

He grinned back at her, more out of reflex than the way he felt. Lane's reaction had really taken his edge off. "Okay," he said, "you got me. It's actually just something I made up to convince my friends that I knew you in a deep and meaningful way."

She shot him a glance of pure disbelief.

"They didn't buy it either," he told her. The drops from her wet body splatted on his cheek. He smiled and wiped them away.

"Hi," Claire said.

"Hi," Hal replied.

"How'd you know I'd be here?"

"Like I said, I knew you couldn't go a whole day without diving."

She looked impressed. "You want to come up?"

Hal climbed the ladder at once and reached the board. He walked toward her, feeling more nervous than he ever had. "Wow. This is some view." He pointed toward the bleachers. "All the cars look so tiny from up here. Hi, tiny cars."

Claire laughed, but she was studying him as he pretended to admire the view. "So why me?"

"Blame it on the bracelet." Hal shrugged. "I'll tell you about it someday."

"I'd like that."

She sat on the diving board and patted a place beside her.

He sat, thinking how the moment should have been so totally cool. Only now it felt just like sitting. They even sat quietly, their legs dangling over the edge of the board, the deep water so far below.

"Hal Brandston," Claire said slowly, testing out the sounds. Then she laughed. "Did you really give mouth-to-mouth resuscitation to a baby chick?"

Hal laughed. "Did Lane tell you that?" He knew it had to have been Lane, and that made him feel confused all over again. "Oh, man. Well, let me tell you what really happened. It was Easter morning, right? And I go over to her house and these baby chicks are, like, croaking all over the place. And there's Lane having a total nervous breakdown." He acted like he was a hero arriving on the scene. "So I *pretended* to give one of these little guys mouth-to-beak to make Lane feel better. She thinks she's so tough, but she's really this complete mushball."

Claire laughed. "Sooooo, anything can happen on a snow day," she said. "That's what you said to me on TV this morning. Is this the *anything* you had in mind?" She leaned in and kissed him softly.

126

He closed his eyes and kissed her back. So many guys would have killed to be in his place. Instead, he sat there and let her kiss him and thought how it wasn't like he'd thought it would be. He kept his eyes closed for a long time after the kiss.

"No," he told her. He was surprised by that answer. She was too; he could see it on her face. "I mean, yes. Believe me. This is more than any *anything* I could have hoped for. It's just . . . it's just not the *anything* that's supposed to happen." And the ache in his heart all of a sudden told him that statement was true. "Oh, man, how could I have been so stupid?"

Claire drew back, confused.

"Not about you, Claire. About Lane."

"Lane," Claire said, understanding more quickly than he had.

"I can't believe what I put her through today. And then when she kissed me . . ."

"She kissed you? What did you do?"

Hal felt very, very stupid. "I, ah, came here."

She shook her head. "Oh, boy. Well I think you know what you have to do."

Hal smiled and nodded. Sudden movement on the ladder drew their attention.

"Hey," Chuck asked, pulling himself up the ladder, "how come no one invited me to the pool party?" He took the ankle bracelet out of his coat pocket and dropped it into Claire's hand. "Here you go, babe. I know how much this bracelet means to you. I thought you might want it back."

"Chuck," Claire said. "Please. Just go back down."

Chuck stepped by her, homing in on Hal. "Sure thing. I'll do that right after I thank Hal for all the joy he's brought me today." He grabbed Hal and put him in a headlock. "Any last words?"

"No," Hal said defiantly.

"I do," Claire spoke up. "When I lost this yesterday, I went crazy looking for it. I've been wearing it for three years." She looked at Hal. "But after today, I realize that I was never supposed to find it. I lost this for a reason, Chuck. And I don't want it back." She wound up to throw the bracelet.

"Claire, no!" Chuck exploded.

"*Sayonara,* Chuck," Claire said. She threw the bracelet into the water.

Chuck let go of Hal and lunged for the bracelet. He lost his balance, then hit the water a second after the bracelet did.

"Nice throw," Hal said.

"Thanks," Claire said, "for everything."

They smiled at each other. Then Hal got moving. Somewhere out there, Lane was wandering around without him. That wasn't right.

Hal found Bill Korn only a short time later. Hal figured Lane would either head to Bill's house or to hers.

Bill was still making snowballs, throwing them into the air, and letting them burst on his forehead. From the slumped and dejected way he was throwing, he didn't appear happy with himself at all.

Hal staggered over, out of breath. "Bill! Bill!"

"Hal?" Bill squinted at him. "Hey, what's up?"

"Not much," Hal told him. "Just running for my life from Chuck." He smiled. "For some strange reason he seems a little irritated with me."

Bill glanced away, looking kind of guilty. "Yeah. He can get kind of grouchy."

"You haven't seen him around, have you?" Hal asked. "He's been doing a pretty good job of finding me today."

Bill looked even more guilty. "Really? He has? Gee. No. I haven't seen him."

"Bill, I need to find Lane. Have you seen her?" Hal asked.

"I saw her about a half hour ago. She was heading for the rink."

"Thanks. You're a real pal," Hal said, already getting into motion. "Now if I can only get there before Chuck gets me."

"Hal, wait. Maybe I can help."

Only a few minutes later, a freeze-dried Chuck found his target near the top of Slupperton Hill. It was bad too, because the poor guy was almost home.

When the guy spotted Chuck on a snowmobile, he froze for just a moment, then started running for all he was worth.

"So this is how it ends." Chuck roared after him on the snowmobile, gaining ground swiftly. Pulling up beside the guy, Chuck threw himself from the snowmobile in a bone-crunching tackle. The guy and Chuck rolled over and down the hill.

When they came to a stop, Chuck landed on top. He rolled his quarry over one more time, turning him face up, and glared down into what he thought would be Hal's face. Chuck drew back a hard-knuckled fist.

"You're not Brandston!" Chuck yelped.

Bill spoke in spite of the fear that filled him. "No, but I'm an incredible simulation."

Chuck shook his head in disbelief. "Where is he, zip? Tell me!"

Bill shook his head.

Chuck smiled evilly. "Then it's your lucky day, because the Chuck Wheeler House of Pain is having a two-for-one offer."

Bill closed his eyes and got himself as ready as he could.

As Chuck prepared for the final act, so did Snowplowman. He was on a plowing rampage. He plowed not only the main roads and thoroughfares but every side street and alley as well. It was as if he was rubbing it in the face of every kid who ever dreamed of a second snow day.

Finally, only one stretch of road remained.

Stubblefield sat behind the snowplow's wheel. "What do you say, Trudy? You want to take it from here?"

Trudy hopped on the steering wheel, then hopped back and forth to steer the big machine.

Natalie stepped out of the shadows into the bright lights of Darling Clementine as the big machine rounded the corner. She stood in the middle of the street, daring Stubblefield to come at her.

There was no question that he was going to do it. It was only a matter of when.

Chapter
19

Natalie stepped out of the shadows and into the headlights of the snowplow so Stubblefield and his bird could clearly see her. She stared through Darling Clementine's windshield and watched as Trudy the parakeet went berserk. She smiled at that, knowing that Snowplowman would only be angrier.

Stubblefield reached for the bird, trying to calm her and hitting the brake at the same time. His voice carried over the open expanse of the unplowed street. "Calm down, girl. That's right. No one's gonna hurt you. Not this time." He stuck his head out the window, glaring at Natalie. "Well, look who's here. If you're waiting for your free plow ride, I'm afraid you'll have to wait until next year. Now get out of my way."

"No," Natalie replied.

"No?" Stubblefield repeated. "You mean no as in

132

'No, Mr. Stubblefield, please don't drive over me like a human speed bump?' "

"No," Natalie shouted back, "as in 'You've stolen your last snow day from us.' "

Stubblefield hopped out of the plow and walked toward her, glancing around. *"Us?* I don't see any *us."* He made a show of looking around. "All I see is a whiny little runt who's going back to school tomorrow."

Pulling Meltar out of her pocket, Natalie held the action figure up so Stubblefield could see it.

"Ooooh," Stubblefield said, "now I'm scared."

"You will be," Natalie stated, "when you"—she changed her voice to Meltar's—"listen to the wind."

Sounds filled the night, loud raucous voices that promised complete and absolute carnage.

"That's not the wind." Stubblefield began to realize in that moment that maybe Natalie *wasn't* alone. Then a hundred and more snow day warriors poured out of the shadows and into the street. They charged Darling Clementine from all directions, carrying ski poles and hockey sticks like swords. Snowballs continually smashed across the cab, caroming in through the snowplow's open window and upsetting Trudy.

"Charge!" Natalie screamed.

Stubblefield's eyes opened in utter shock. He tried to run back to the snowplow and get under way, but there were kids everywhere. All of them were out to get revenge for all the lost snow days, all the things

133

that might have been for a magical day that had slipped through their fingers.

In the midst of the ambush, Chet stepped up onto a hill and pulled the disgusting yellow snowball from his pocket. "Like they say, don't eat yellow snow." He wound up to throw.

"Wait," Wayne said. "He's mine."

Chet handed the snowball over and Wayne let it rip.

Stubblefield tried to make it back to the snowplow's cab while being assaulted with a hundred snowballs. Then the yellow snowball slammed into his face, knocking him down. He got up and tried for the snowplow again. He almost made it, but then two kids on sleds zipped by with a trip rope stretched between them. The rope caught Snowplowman at his ankles, knocking him to the ground. The kids tied Snowplowman to a Caution, School Zone sign with his own jumper cables. He struggled to free himself, with no luck. Then, as the kids taunted him, he realized something.

"Ha-ha," Stubblefield exploded. "Ha-ha-ha. I'm sorry, but it is funny. You dimwits thinking you've clobbered me when the truth is, I've already won!"

All the laughing and jeering that had been going on around him kind of died away.

"That's right!" Stubblefield continued. "Look around. So what if I don't plow this street. All the others are clear. See you in school tomorrow."

Almost dead silence filled the street around him.

Stubblefield grinned. "Never thought of that, did you?"

"Actually," Natalie said, "we did." She waved, and Chet stepped out of Darling Clementine with keys in his hand. The kids all burst out in louder laughter than ever before.

"Anyone want to go for a ride?" Chet said.

"Noooo!" Stubblefield yelled in real terror. "You can't take Clementine!"

Wayne stepped forward, then started singing. "She was lost and gone forever—"

"—dreadful sorrow, Clementine!" the rest of the kids chimed in on cue.

"Sorry we can't stay and chitchat, but we've got a lot of unplowing to do." Natalie led the way back to the snowplow. Kids piled into the snowplow, whooping and hollering.

Natalie ground the gears, and the snowplow lurched into motion. She drove toward the snowbanks piled high on the side of the street. She used the blade control to position the blade properly, then started pushing the snow back onto the street.

Lashed to a sign pole, staggering down the street, Stubblefield fell on an icy patch. He couldn't get back up. He had no choice but to watch as the polar explorer kid trudged into view, pulling his sled.

The polar explorer kid stared at him with concern. Trudy was perched on his shoulder. "Admunson! What the blazes? I was on my way to the pole when I found your bird. Thought you might be in a spot of trouble." He chuckled. "My, you are in quite a pickle, aren't you?"

Stubblefield snarled, "Just untie me, you worm."

"Why should I?"

"Because," Stubblefield thought quickly, "I . . . I can help you."

"You?"

"Sure." Stubblefield tried a smile. "Not many people know this, but I've always wanted to be an explorer myself."

The polar explorer looked excited. He started cutting Stubblefield loose. "Is that so? Well, to be honest with you, Admunson, I could use the help. Roscoe, I'm afraid, has seen better days."

"Well then," Stubblefield said, "to the top of the world!" When the ropes dropped away, he stood and laughed in the kid's face. "On second thought, I think I'll go look for my truck. Maybe stomp on a few kids along the way." He took Trudy from the kid's shoulder.

The polar explorer gave him a disgusted look. "Fine. Go. Return to the sorry mess you call your life."

Stubblefield halted, then turned around. The kid had struck a nerve. "What do you know about my life?"

"I know that you got lost somewhere along the way. Come with me, Admunson. It's not too late."

"Oh would you just cut the act?" Stubblefield yelled. "There is no pole. You're no explorer. And guess what? I'm not Admunson."

"No," the kid said quietly, "you're wrong. You're just too much of a fool to know it."

Stubblefield remained quiet. So much had happened in the last few hours. He stood there and continued thinking, more than he'd thought in years.

Darling Clementine kept clunking along. The streets behind them were all plowed back over so they'd be pretty much impassable.

"Hey, Natalie, isn't that your brother?" Wayne asked when he spotted Hal's clothes trying to make their way home.

She peered through the darkness, still ticked at her brother. She rolled down the window. "Losers walk!"

Bill, still dressed in Hal's clothes and having just been given the full tour of Chuck Wheeler's House of Pain, tried to turn around but lost his balance and fell into the snow.

At first, all the riders in the snowplow thought it was a great stunt. It wasn't until Natalie glanced in the rearview mirror and saw that it was Bill Korn dressed in her brother's clothes that she stopped.

Darling Clementine ground to a stop in the middle of the street.

"Man-oh-man-oh-Manhattan clam chowder," Wayne said.

For the first time that day, Natalie got really worried about her brother. They got out of the snowplow. "Bill," Natalie said, "what happened? Where's Hal?"

"I didn't tell him," Bill said. "Chuck wanted to know, but I didn't tell him."

Natalie swapped looks with the other kids, totally lost. "Bill," she said, "where is Hal?"

Hal stood in the shadows near Crowley Rink watching Lane as she skated by herself. He wondered why he had never noticed how beautiful she looked. Actually, he guessed he had noticed it, just not in this way. Memory of that kiss she'd given him burned in his mind.

Gray clouds streamed from his mouth as he tried to catch his breath. He'd run the whole way, pushing himself to exhaustion. He drew in a deep breath, doubling over from all the effort. "Lane!" he yelled, hoping she'd hear. He really didn't think he had the strength to go even that much farther. "Lane! Hey, Lane!"

An Al Martino record played inside the rink, and he knew that there was no way Lane was going to hear him over the music. He started forward again, ignoring the pain in his side and concentrating on the pain in his heart. He hadn't thought he could ever hurt Lane so bad, or allow anyone else to, either.

Before he made it to the rink, someone tapped him on the shoulder.

When Hal turned around, Chuck Wheeler's fist smashed into his face.

Chapter 20

Hal went backward from the force of Chuck Wheeler's blow, ending up on his back in the snow. Dazed, he flailed around weakly, feeling like a bug on a specimen board that wasn't quite dead. He couldn't get up.

It wouldn't have mattered anyway. Chuck would have put him back down. Chuck stepped forward, lifted a big boot, and planted it on Hal's bleeding nose.

"To help stop the bleeding," Chuck said, grinning, his face looking harsher than ever in the shadows, "apply pressure directly on the wound."

With his boot on Hal's nose, Hal honked like a duck when he spoke. "What's . . . your . . . problem? Nothing happened with me and Claire. *Nothing.*"

Chuck leaned harder on his foot, making Hal

think he was going to put his nose through the back of his head. "Gee, what a surprise. Of *course* nothing happened. She was playing you to get back at me. That performance at the pool . . . stellar. She almost had me going."

Hal grabbed Chuck's boot and tried to remove it from his face. But after a little while he was convinced the only way it was coming off was through laser surgery. "Yeah," he said out of spite, "especially the part where she threw the bracelet into the pool."

Chuck stepped down harder. "She'd never leave me. What do you know about anything?"

Hal looked at him, straining to keep his voice steady enough to be heard. "What color are her eyes, Chuck?"

Moving in an explosion of power, Chuck reached down and grabbed the front of Bill's snowsuit, yanking Hal almost effortlessly to his feet. He pulled Hal's face close to his, breathing on him.

Hal's eyes widened in surprise, and he was sure Chuck thought it was because he was afraid of him. Actually, Hal spotted Darling Clementine rumbling into the skating rink's parking lot. Hal couldn't hear the snowplow over the rumbling of Chuck's snowmobile, so he guessed Chuck couldn't either. Hal had no idea what Stubblefield was doing there.

"Like I'm really going to tell you," Chuck sneered. "I know her, you waste-case. I know her better than anybody."

Hal couldn't help looking past Chuck at Darling

140

Clementine. The snowplow hadn't changed course at all. He figured he must have taken a pretty hard shot from Chuck because he could have sworn he saw Natalie behind the wheel instead of Stubblefield.

"I can't believe I'm even talking to you," Chuck stated. "You're a zero. You're nothing. You're invisible."

Hal looked at the snowplow again. That *was* Natalie behind the wheel, and Wayne and Chet were in the cab with her, along with a lot of other kids. He couldn't believe Chuck hadn't heard the growling engine racing toward them, but he had his snowmobile helmet on too.

Natalie lowered Darling Clementine's plow blade, and snow erupted from the parking lot, peeling over to the side in an avalanche.

"I'm not sure I'm following you," Hal told Chuck in an effort to gain time.

Chuck's face purpled with rage. "You are a zip," he screamed. "You go out with other zips. I'm Chuck Wheeler. I go out with Claire Bonner." He pulled back a fist to paste Hal again, but by then the snowplow was almost on top of them.

"Yeah," Hal replied cockily, "Well, not technically." He was still winded and still hurting, but the sight of that big machine rushing toward them whipping up its own winter war just flooded his adrenaline glands. He tore loose from Chuck's grip and dived out of the way.

Chuck turned, thinking he was going after Hal. Then he saw Darling Clementine practically on top of him. Hal decided that seeing the way Chuck's eyes tried to pop out of his head was worth getting his nose mashed. Chuck tried to run, but it was too late. The plow blade caught him up in the tidal wave of snow it pushed ahead.

One second Chuck Wheeler was standing there. In the next, he was buried in a huge heap of snow on the other side of the parking lot.

Hal staggered to his feet, listening to Chuck's pained groans coming from somewhere inside the mini-mountain of snow. Hal couldn't help it; he smiled. "Unbelievable."

When Darling Clementine rolled back to Hal's side like a sedate puppy, Natalie was hanging out the window. She smiled devilishly.

"Nats," Hal called up to her.

"Hal," she called back.

"You totally saved my butt. He was going to kill me. He . . . You're driving Snowplowman's truck."

"Remember this morning when I said I didn't need you today?" she asked.

Hal nodded. "I guess you weren't kidding."

Natalie raised her eyebrows. "So what happened with that girl, Claire?"

Hal didn't feel like going into it just then because he still hadn't finished with it. Lane was still on the ice, skating to cheesy tunes. "Let's just say something else came up." He glanced over at the rink where he could still see Lane skating. She didn't even know anything had happened.

"Was it worth wasting your whole day for?"

"I hope so," Hal said, "I know that's not what you wanted to hear, but the thing is, for me right now, I guess there are more important things than saving the universe." He paused. "You'll understand in about . . . hmmm . . . say, three years."

Natalie smiled, starting to understand. "That's okay. Meltar and I can take care of the universe, no problem." She held up Meltar. "Oh, um, I borrowed him. Don't worry. I didn't scratch him or anything. Here, you can have him back." She started to toss Meltar down.

Hal shook his head, making a decision. "It's all right. The Questmaster belongs to you now. You've earned him."

Natalie smiled.

"Just be careful," Hal said. "There's a lot of bad out there." He nodded at Chuck, who'd finally managed to stand up.

Natalie nodded. "Well, we should go. We've got a lot of unplowing to do."

Hal waved good-bye as Natalie threw the big machine into gear again. "See you at the house."

Then Hal turned back around and yelled out to his sister before she got too far away. "Nats, if by some miracle it turns out that there's another snow day tomorrow, I was wondering . . . you doing anything?"

She smiled at him. Then she and her wrecking crew headed out to destroy everything Snowplowman had accomplished.

Hal entered the skating rink and walked over to

the railing. He sat down on a bench. Sitting there in the shadows, Hal knew Lane couldn't see him. But he could see her. He started forward, and Lane saw him.

Immediately she turned and started to skate away.

Hal went after her, his boots slipping on the ice. "Lane, wait!" he yelled. "Please. We have to talk." He took off after her, but he was still somewhat loopy from Chuck's punch and not having skates didn't help at all.

"Why aren't you with Miss Fantasy Girl?" she asked. "Did she shoot you down? Gee. What a surprise."

"No," Hal replied. "That's not what happened. Come on. Wait up."

"Go away. I have nothing to say to you."

"Will you listen?" Hal said. "Before . . . when you kissed me—"

"No! Don't! I don't want to talk about that! Ever!" Lane skated even faster, much too fast for him to keep up.

Hal tried to get around the sick feeling in his head as he struggled to put on more speed. "Just hear me"—without warning, he lost his balance and fell— "oooouuuuuttt!"

He turned into a flailing heap, skidding across the ice. He slammed into the boards by the railing with a bone-jarring thump. He groaned and lay there, too far gone to ever move again. At least that was how he felt at that particular moment.

"Ooooooh," he groaned in faked pain.

Lane skated over to look down at him.

"My spine," Hal wheezed. "Can't feel my legs. Help me, Lane. Help . . . me."

She shook her head in disbelief. "You're pathetic."

Hal lunged quickly, grabbing her ankles. She almost fell. "And yet," he said, "it would seem that it is you who has the reflexes of a dead cow."

She finally lost the war against gravity and imbalance and fell. "Haaaallll!" she screamed. They wrestled on the ice, and she quickly gained the upper hand, pinning him down.

"All right," Hal said, laughing. "All right. You win. You win."

Lane's smile slowly faded. "Hal, what are you doing here? What do you want? What . . . what is all this?"

Hal looked into her eyes. "Wasn't it you who said that true love's all about finding someone you can stand to be with for ten minutes at a time?"

"Yeah." She looked at him, so many questions in her eyes.

"You got ten minutes?" Hal asked. He leaned in and kissed her. She didn't kiss back. At least she didn't kiss back at first, but then she did. And Hal could think of no better place in the whole world to be.

You never really know how a snow day is going to turn out, but by the time the sun goes down you might be amazed to discover that you won the race to the pole. . . .

The polar explorer kid struggled to plant his flag on top of Slupperton Hill. Roger Stubblefield reached out and helped him, then looked around quickly to make sure no one was watching. He stepped back and saluted.

You got to wear pants again. . . .

Tom Brandston, dressed in a nice suit, stood in front of a satellite weather photo and read the forecast.

You got your life back . . .

Laura and Randy sat on the stoop eating icicles.

Or not.

Principal Weaver stumbled into his house and locked the door behind him. He was worn out and grimy. He let out a sigh of relief.
Then he got slammed by a hundred snowballs inside his own house. He went down, but they kept hitting him.

And in the end you might even discover that you saved the universe.

Natalie, Meltar, and the rest of her friends drove Darling Clementine down snow-filled streets.

*   *   *

Hal held Lane as they skated. Both of them wore goofy smiles.

And even though the snow will melt and the schools will open and everything will go back to normal, the day that began with a single perfect snowflake will stay with you forever.

About the Author

MEL ODOM lives in Moore, OK, where snow days are rare and always filled with magic. Thankfully, he gets to visit Minnesota for Christmases with his wife and children, where snow is white and fluffy and snowball fights and sled rides are never out of the question. He is the author of several books based on the television shows *Buffy the Vampire Slayer; Sabrina, the Teenage Witch; The Journey of Allen Strange; The Secret World of Alex Mack;* and *Young Hercules*. He enjoys correspondence, and readers can send him e-mail at denimbyte@aol.com.